SHORTS

A Collection of Short Stories

by

Lawrence V. Drake

www.drakeip.com

Edited by: Lawrence V. Drake, Teresa L. Drake

Cover designed by Lawrence Drake

ISBN:

www.drakeip.com

Table of Contents

Lawrence V. Drake has been published in dozens of periodicals, authored memoirs and novels, written industry-related books, and penned a monthly international newsletter. He has been a pilot for most of his life, owning and flying a variety of sport and private aircraft.

Born and raised in Montana, Lawrence has lived all over the western U.S. In his early years, he worked as a flight instructor, crop duster, and an aerobatic instructor, owning and flying a variety of airplanes including antiques and amateur-built. His memoir, Schellville, captures those adventure-filled days.

Almost four years in the Air Force Security Service during the Vietnam conflict gave rise to his first book, Red Boots Rebel. His second book, The Entrepreneur Experience, is a result of a lifetime of educational encounters with dreamers, schemers, and scalawags as an independent entrepreneur. He spent much of his career in the construction industry as a manufacturer, association director, and business owner. He holds a number of patents, including a unique modular RV camper and portable shelter.

Lawrence writes from a first-hand perspective of a love of aviation, an entrepreneur, a caring family man, and a passion for life.

Since "retirement" I have been busier than I have ever been. I call it retirement because, in 2009 I left the organization that I had built over a fifteen year period; one that had provided a steady income, although tentative at times. I intended to simplify my life. Instead, I started a new business, wrote books, developed software, and websites, produced videos, and generally created a whole new set of complications. I hope that you might find something here that interests you.

— Lawrence V. Drake

BOOKS BY LAWRENCE V. DRAKE

Pilots & Painted Ladies: 493rd Bomb Squadron and the Air War in the CBI

Schellville: The Aviator and the Hippie

Red Boots Rebel: Keeping Secrets

When Silence Calls: Freeing the Island Deaf

The Entrepreneur Experience: Good Choices and Common Mistakes

Visit DrakeIP.com or scan the code below.

The Bonneville

Not long after Dad purchased his new, slightly used 1959 Pontiac Bonneville, he handed me the keys and said, "here, Son, pickup the horse trailer at the ranch and take it over to the Hagstrom's place."

"Me? I get to drive the Pontiac? By myself?"

"Think you can handle it?"

"And pull the horse trailer?"

"You've done it with me several times. Just

be careful."

Now, that represented an amazing display of confidence in his eighteen-year-old son. Particularly since Dad took great pride in his gleaming, forest green sedan with its twin rocket fins streaming back over space-age taillights. The car looked fast just sitting there. This wouldn't be my first venture out in the car but the occasions were rare and I had never pulled a trailer.

The family ranch sat below the rimrock bluffs ten miles west of town. We called it the "ranch" although it consisted of nothing more than some rolling hills, a small pole barn, and a corral for our three horses. Dad acquired the ranch to live out his secret life as a cowboy when not heading up his architectural firm. We had an old one-horse trailer for transporting a steed to various events. Not exactly a ranch vehicle, the Bonneville did the job of towing for now. Dad really needed a pickup to complete his persona. That would come later.

What is a teenage boy supposed to do when presented with such an opportunity? First and foremost, the adventure needed to be shared.

"Hey, Mike. I got my Dad's car. Want to go

for a ride?"

My best friend, Mike Bissell never turned down an invitation to get out of the house. He knew immediately that going for a ride had potential. "Sure thing. What's up?"

I explained the errand I had been asked to run and said I would be over in a few minutes to pick him up. When I arrived at his house looking as cool as I could behind the wheel of the Pontiac, he jumped up from the porch steps, swung open the gate-sized door of my beautiful sedan, and hopped into the passenger seat.

"Can we pick up Sue? She said she'd like to come along, too"

Mike and his recently acquired girlfriend made a good couple. They both had a great sense of humor and kept each other laughing continuously. I felt a little jealous when they started hanging out together. It cut into my buddy time. I liked Sue a lot but she now seemed to be included in most everything Mike and I did.

"Sure. Why not?" And, so as not to be the third wheel, I said, "I want to stop by and see if Karla wants to join us, too."

I had met Karla through my younger

brother's girlfriend a few weeks earlier. A stunning girl with Hollywood features and a warm, down-to-earth personality, Karla was way out of my league. Somehow, I had managed to make friends with her. It helped that I held the prestige of being a graduated senior. That put me in the "older man" category and Karla was clearly more mature than her male high school classmates. Age does have its advantages. Just maybe, a ride in a late model Pontiac Bonneville would sway her affections in my direction.

As Mike and Sue gave moral support from the car window, I rang Karla's doorbell. She answered.

"Hi, Karla. Mike, Sue, and I are heading out to my ranch to pick up a horse trailer. Wanna come with us?" I tried hard to sound confident, and not reveal that my heart bounced around in my chest like a basketball being dribbled.

Karla peeked over my shoulder and waved at the couple in the car. "Okay, sounds like fun."

"Really? Great." I may have sounded a little more surprised than I should have.

"I'll just grab some things and be right out."

I walked back to the car a bit taller.

What could be better? A beautiful girl at my side, my buddy and his sweetie in the back, warm weather, and clear blue skies. The day was made for adventure.

A quick stop at the A&W Drive-In for refreshments and the drive to the ranch passed quickly with laughs and giggles all around. Displaying expert proficiency, I backed the Pontiac up to the trailer, hooked it up to the hitch, tightened the ball knob, attached the safety chains, and checked the lights. All passed my inspection under the watchful eyes of my passengers. Hopefully, they were as impressed as I was.

The Bonneville pulled the empty trailer with ease as we bumped over the dirt road leading out of the ranch property. Once on the pavement, I could hardly tell it trailed behind. I nonchalantly monitored my progress in the rearview mirrors, careful to avoid telegraphing my nervousness. Meanwhile, teenage bantering and laughter filled the car. Karla seemed to genuinely enjoy my company. Her smile and beauty captivated me.

We arrived at the Hagstrom's property without incident. I had driven flawlessly and the tension of towing would soon be over. I backed the trailer into its spot in a single try beside some other equipment on a small incline.

"Wow, nice job," Mike complimented. "I couldn't do that."

I didn't tell him that it was a first for me. The few times I had done it before took several attempts. Backing a trailer was not easy.

With the trailer now in its new home, I cranked down the tongue wheel, loosened the ball knob, unplugged the lights, and lifted the trailer tongue off of the car hitch.

"A job well done," I announced. "Now it's time to party."

Free of that anchor, I planned to get the full benefit of this opportune freedom.

As we pulled away down the hill, I glanced again in the rearview mirror to admire my handiwork. "Holy cow!"

Following close behind and gaining fast, the trailer grew large. Out of complete surprise, I did the only thing that occurred to me at that moment. I slammed on the brakes. Two seconds later the car lurched forward to the sickening bang and the sound of crunching metal as the tongue of the trailer pierced the beautiful chrome grillwork decorating the trunk of the Bonneville.

"Yikes. What was that?" Mike yelped as the girls squealed.

I slammed the shifter into park. Mike and I jumped out to survey the damage while our dates stared out the rear window. The trailer tongue had struck dead center, impaling itself into the trunk, punching through the chrome letter 'T" in Pontiac. My stomach sank to my toes. What had gone wrong? I know I had decoupled the trailer.

"The safety chains," Mike exclaimed, pointing at the offending metallic links still attached to the car hitch. "You didn't unhook the chains."

"Oh, man," I exclaimed, grabbing my head. "Dad's going to kill me. How could I be so stupid? How am I gonna explain this?"

"Well," Mike rubbed the back of his neck while studying the steel beam disappearing into the trunk. "First, you have to figure out how to get it out of there."

I glanced at the concerned faces peering out the rear window and for the first time felt my face getting flush from embarrassment. I quickly looked back at the scene of the accident, my mind racing for a solution.

"Find some big rocks and put them in front of the tires," I directed.

Big rocks were not hard to find between the sagebrush and the yucca plants on the hill. Mike quickly had placed one large stone under each wheel of the trailer. I crouched down and unhooked the offending chains.

"I should be able to move the car forward now and leave the trailer behind. You watch and let me know if it starts moving."

The girls sat silently as I put the Pontiac in gear and inched forward. My plan worked. With some squeaks and squeals, the car disengaged itself from the violating spear.

"Look at that," Mike said. "It made a perfectly square hole."

With the car stopped, I walked around to see an opening about four inches square that could have been made in a machine shop. "Hoooo, boy..."

We hooked the trailer back up properly and returned it to its place on the hill. This time, three attempts were required to get it backed in straight. The rocks went back under the wheels, and every possible connection to the car was checked and rechecked to make certain it wouldn't be following us again.

Settled back in the car, I resolved not to let the event completely ruin our day. “Well, what’s done is done. Since I can’t do anything about it, what do you say we take a little drive? I know a back way to the top of the rimrocks.”

Everyone seemed in agreement, so off we went, determined to enjoy the rest of our outing.

The road I had chosen to get us to the top turned out to be a two-track, rain-rutted, dirt trail that should not be attempted by anything less than a Jeep or a pickup. Unfortunately, I had been with Dad on several occasions when he took off cross-country through the brambles in the family sedan at the ranch. He obviously had better judgment than me when it came to off-road terrain. I lacked his skill but I wasn’t about to back down and admit that once I started up the trail.

We bounced around wildly, laughing hard at each jarring as the Bonneville bravely scaled the ever-increasingly rough and steep track. Then, with one loud thud, the low-slung auto smacked down hard onto a small boulder exposed by rain erosion. An ear-piercing, high-pitched whistling ‘zinnnng...zinnng’ ensued with every rev of the engine. I stopped the car and sat mortified.

Stupid, stupid, stupid... ran through my brain as I felt three pairs of eyes focusing on me. I did the only thing I could. I slowly climbed out, crouched down, and peered under the car, hoping to not see a puddle of oil mixed with the dust.

“No oil... that’s good,” I said half whispering. “Looks like the oil pan has been smashed into the flywheel.” I wanted to at least sound like I knew what I was talking about.

“Do you think we can make it home?” Karla asked.

No one doubted that our joyride had ended.

“I hope so.” I started the engine. ‘zinnng...zinng’ At least the engine was running.

At that point, I didn’t even want to think of how I was going to explain all this to Dad. I just wanted to get everyone home and end the nightmare. I slowly backed down the trail until I found a wide spot to turn around. Only small conversations took place as I made the rounds dropping my friends off. The constant whistling of the damage made talking difficult.

“Sorry it turned out so bad,” Karla offered. “We still had some fun, didn’t we?”

I said goodbye, wondering if I would ever have the courage to call her again.

"I hope you don't get in too much trouble," Sue consoled as she waved goodbye at the curb.

"What are you going to do now?" Mike queried. "Sure am glad I'm not in your shoes."

The drive back had given me plenty of time to think. The hole in the trunk was almost forgivable. Surely, I wasn't the first guy to forget to disconnect the safety chains. That one would be fairly easy to explain. After all, it happened while doing the job he sent me to do—a dumb accident. On the other hand, how could I justify a bashed-in oil pan? That would lead to embarrassing questions that I didn't want to answer. Where did it happen? What were you doing? Were you alone? I imagined sweating under the hot lights of interrogation.

"I have an idea for the oil pan. I'm going to take the car to my uncle's shop. Maybe he can fix it so at least I won't have to explain that to Dad."

Mike's forehead wrinkled, "won't he tell your father?"

"Maybe...but maybe not. Uncle Ed got into more than his share of trouble. From what I hear, he was kind of a rowdy kid. If he can fix it, he might cover for me."

"Good luck. Let me know what happens."

"Okay, I will. That is if I'm ever let out of the house again."

Heads turned as the Bonneville whistled its way through the city streets en route to the shop. I pulled through the alley into the back lot and quickly shut down. I found my uncle working on a radiator.

"Hi, Uncle Ed."

"Oh, hi, Larry. What are you doing here?"

"Well... I have sort of a problem I'm hoping you can help me with."

"Yeah, what's that?"

I carefully launched into my tale of woe, revealing only the minimum details as to how it all happened. I avoided any reference to my passengers. If done right, I figured I might be able to make it sound like I was doing Dad a favor by bringing the car in for repair.

A knowing smile hid behind Uncle Ed's concerned look as he listened. I think he knew there was more to my story. There seemed to be an unspoken understanding of my plight.

"Go bring it in," he said calmly. "I'll run 'er up on the rack and see what I can do."

The high pitch whistle echoed through the

shop as I drove up onto the lift. I shut down, got out, and stood aside as the lift hoisted the car into the air. My legs quivered and my heart pounded in my ears. Surely, there would be a mangled mess underneath requiring hours of work and piles of money for parts.

Ed flipped on his inspection light and surveyed the scene for several minutes.

"You lucked out. It's just a small dent—an easy fix. I don't see any real damage. I'll have you out of here in no time."

"Really!" Warmth spread throughout my body as it relaxed after being tense for so long. "Wow! Thank you."

Within twenty minutes, the car was off the rack and back in the parking lot, purring like a kitten. Uncle Ed must have known how worried I was. As I got ready to leave he leaned into the window.

"You take it easy now. No more jeep trails."

"No, sir!"

"Say hi to your folks for me." He patted the side of the car and sent me on my way.

I drove slowly and carefully on the way home, not in a hurry to face my father.

Dad surprised me and took the news of the trailer puncture in stride. I wasn't grounded or denied access to the family car. Evidently, he had forgotten to unhook the chains a time or two himself, albeit without the resulting bone-jarring impact. The body shop restored the trunk to its original space-age look and Dad didn't mention the incident again. My guilty conscience provided plenty of punishment for my deceit and served to deter me from attempting similar follies in the future. I never knew if Uncle Ed revealed his part in my cover-up but every once in a while I caught a twinkle and a smile from him at family gatherings.

Dead Critter Ranch

I am one who believes that houses are built for humans, not animals. That belief has often put me in conflict with my family and friends, particularly those who are partial to dogs. That having been said, I found it hard to resist the pleadings of my three young daughters and their mother to acquire a puppy.

"Can we get a puppy? We'll take care of it and clean up after it. We promise. You won't have to do anything.... so, please... please... please!"

After a few weeks of such begging, against my better judgment, I finally succumbed to their feminine will.

"Well, if I let you have a puppy, it will have to stay out of the house. It'll be an outdoor dog."

"Oh, yes, Daddy. Thank you, thank you, thank you."

"And it will have to be a small dog. I don't want a big mutt that will drop piles in the yard, and eat us out of house and home. But, no yappers either. I can't handle yappers."

"We'll find just the right one," my wife said assuredly.

"Remember, girls, a dog is a long term commitment. You can't just decide one day you don't want to take care of it anymore," I lectured.

I immediately had second thoughts about my approval but the die was cast. I watched as my ecstatic little family headed down the driveway of our small hobby farm in search of their new love. A few hours later they returned, smiling and giggling. As they walked toward the house, to my surprise the two younger girls were each carrying a small ball of fur. My wife wore a rather sheepish look of guilt.

"Two dogs!" I exhaled in disbelief. "You got two dogs."

"But they're small," my wife pleaded in her defense. "And they are brothers. We couldn't separate brothers."

"Small!" I cried out. "Yeah, they're small now... they're puppies. Look at those paws... they're huge. These guys will turn into big dogs."

"No, they won't. They're huskies and huskies aren't that big."

"Huskies! You've got to be kidding me!"

I could have marched them all right back to the car and sent them back where they got the dogs, but the look of pure joy in my daughter's eyes was too much for any father to overcome. The puppies stayed. They found a home in the corner of the garage for a while, but it wasn't long before dad had to build a kennel, and dad had to install a doggy door from the garage into the kennel, and dad had to build a doghouse. Soon the dogs grew from adorable little fuzz balls to teenage dogs that shed like crazy, ate everything in sight, and left large piles of poop.

One other thing I hadn't anticipated. These two brothers, now named Sully and Kiowa, became escape artists. They could climb fences, chew through plywood, rip holes in chain link, and defy any form of containment I could devise. I tried the invisible fence with the wire buried around the perimeter of the yard and shock collars on the dogs. The collars were totally ineffective until their thick fur had been shaved away to allow the collars to contact their skin. They definitely felt the shock. The two would approach the boundary, share a "this is going to hurt" look, then bound across the barrier with a yelp and be off on the hunt.

Huskies are runners and hunters. Fortunately, we lived in the country with acres upon acres of wooded area. A creek ran through the lower part that provided muskrats, rabbits, squirrels and plenty of other prey for the two energetic hounds. As penance for escaping, they would deposit the trophies of their hunt on our front lawn and porch. Our cemetery of carcasses grew almost daily and I got tired of digging holes. The UPS driver who visited our home regularly referred to our place as "The Dead Critter Ranch."

I thought things had got completely out of hand when the dogs showed up one day with the hindquarter of a cow. Where and how they had come by it, I have no idea. I had to come up with a way to contain these two creatures. In the meantime, they continued to defy my attempts. One Sunday morning I opened the front door to find the neighbor's white American rabbit in a heap on the porch, the one their daughter had won first prize with at the county fair. The neighbors had not been pleased with Sully and Kiowa's almost daily romps through their place but until now, had not caused any real problems. How they had got the rabbit out of its hutch was a mystery, but being masters at breaking out, breaking in would be no challenge.

I didn't relish the idea of presenting a dirty, dead prize bunny with the accompanying humble apologies. If I simply buried the thing, I'm sure our neighbors would have their suspicions. I looked over the rabbit and found no bleeding or punctures. It was just dirty. Then the thought struck me. What if I cleaned it up and put it back in the cage. They were gone to church this morning. Maybe they would think it died of natural causes. Sometimes irrational plans sound good in times of stress.

I carried the dead animal to the utility sink, broke out the shampoo and lathered it up. Once clean, the hair dryer fluffed up its fur nicely. The big white rabbit lay there looking as though it were quietly napping. This could work.

Making sure the neighbor's SUV was gone, I crept through the trees and into their back yard to the rabbit hutches. The deceased rabbit's hutch was unlatched but with no other sign of a break-in. I wondered how those guys got in. I placed the big bunny on the straw, arranging him in a comfortable position, locked the cage, and made my way home without being caught. Success!

The next day, I met Brian, our neighbor at the mailboxes where we exchanged the usual pleasantries. "Hi, how are you. Nice day."

"Did you have a nice weekend?" I casually asked, certain I had gotten away with my plan.

"Well, you know the strangest thing happened. Our prize-winning American rabbit died the other day so we had a little funeral and I buried it. Then Sunday afternoon I go out to feed the others and I found it back in its cage!"

Buggy Blues

He could have raised his bid and won the clean little horse-drawn doctor's buggy at Ray's Auction Barn, but Vernon let it pass—just a bit too expensive. A year ago, he came up with the notion to join the 1982 Centennial Wagon Train reenactment from Fort Smith to

Billings, Montana. That instigated a search for a rig and a horse to pull it. He came up empty-handed until he and his wife made a trip to visit their daughter in Indiana.

Being involved in the farming community, his son-in-law took Vernon and Bettie to a farm sale where there happened to be the prettiest little black buggy with a fold-down canvas top and large yellow wheels—and going for bottom dollar.

"I'm going to buy that," he told his wife.

"Really?" Bettie said in disbelief. "Aren't you putting the cart before the horse?"

"But look, it's a beauty."

"How are you going to pay for it—use my new carpet money?"

Vernon didn't listen. He was too focused on the prize.

"How are you going to get it home? In our airline luggage?"

Vernon didn't consider the two thousand mile trip home a problem, only a challenge.

A few phone calls eliminated crating and shipping as being too expensive—the same for renting a U-Haul truck.

"I've got a utility trailer you can have," Vernon's son-in-law offered.

Vernon quipped. "I'll buy a pickup, load the buggy on the trailer, and we'll tow it home."

Bettie could see he set his mind, so off they went to the farm sale and wrote the check for $950. Vernon became the proud owner of a vintage doctor's buggy, complete with harness and tack. Now he needed a pickup to pull his prize home and a horse to pull it when he got there.

A bit of shopping around produced a nice 1972 El Camino for $6,000, plus hitch, plus tarp, plus license, and insurance. Not a real pickup, Chevrolet made a two-door station wagon into a sporty utility vehicle with a built-in cargo bed.

"Not to worry, Bettie, I'll sell it when we get home and make a couple hundred in profit."

"Should our new carpet be off-white or rust," she asked.

Vernon got off the phone after talking to the airline. "Ah, well, no refund on our return airline tickets. There goes the profit on the pickup."

With the buggy in tow, the couple headed out for the long trip to Montana. All too soon it became obvious that towing proved to be a big job for the little pickup. At fifteen miles per gallon and three stops for repairs to get it to run right, the expenses piled up. By the time they got to South Dakota, snow flew over the windshield. Passing through Sturgis, ice on a bridge sent them into the guardrail, wiping out the side of the El Camino and throwing a scare into the couple. After assessing the damage, Vernon pronounced the pickup still drivable. Shaky from their ordeal, they safely made the rest of the way home, albeit with a slightly less attractive vehicle.

The repair cost of the bridge encounter came to $1,400. Then there was the valve job on the engine. The El Camino remained in the shop with no idea of what that bill would be. The bargain-priced buggy lost its luster long ago. Bettie got her $2,200 off-white carpet but the faded sofa looked out of place, so a thousand dollars upholstery job fixed that. Unfortunately, the wallpaper no longer matched the sofa and needed to be extended into the dining room.

In exchange for a birthday gift of a two-wheel driving harness from Bettie and daughters, Vernon felt obliged to agree to new drapes, curtains, two occasional chairs, and a coffee table, with a new bedroom set thrown in for good measure.

A buggy is no good without a horse to pull it. Undaunted, Vernon found a beautiful Tennessee Walker mare named Donna-Far-Go. For $2,000, plus the cost of new horseshoes, he obtained the other half of his buggy combo. Never mind that Donna-Far-Go had never been in harness, let alone pulled anything.

After six short weeks of training with the driving harness, Vernon got the horse to go in the general direction he wanted when commanded, although she didn't like the idea of stopping, standing, or backing. In any event, the time came to join the Wagon Train snaking through the hills of Eastern Montana on its way to Billings. An investment in food, supplies, and horse trailer rental further added to the growing tally. All were loaded and hauled into the country where the Wagon Train camped for the night.

Vernon hitched Donna-Far-Go to the buggy containing all his camping supplies and led her to the gate in the fence where the entire train previously passed through that morning as it made its way down the valley. The Walker decided she didn't want to go through and reared up in the harness taking Vernon's arm with her, giving him a mighty jerk. He fell face-forward and landed directly under the dancing hooves of the spooked horse. Slightly trampled and an aching shoulder, he pulled himself up and regained control of the animal.

Now, with one arm barely functional, determination drove him not to miss the chance of a lifetime. Putting the pain aside, he got his rig through the gate and onto the trail. As the train slowly made its way across the far side of the valley, a small black buggy pulled by a horse that neither knew how to walk slow, stop or back up, could be seen making rapid circles around and around at the tail end of the train. For the next four days, Vernon and his buggy traveled ten times the miles of the wagon train as he labored with his one good arm to rein in his over-enthusiastic steed.

After lost ropes, several repairs to a broken harness, rain, mud, cold, and a cookstove that wouldn't heat the beef stew, Vernon pulled in west of Billings with the rest of the train, tired and sore but gratified that he made the trip and fulfilled his dream.

The next day the Wagon Train joined the Western Day Parade through downtown, Vernon and his buggy once again taking up the rear. With a bandaged arm and a helping of pain pills, he worked to control his fine Tennessee Walker. The weary traveler tallied the cost of his adventure as the crowd cheered the end of the parade. All told, he figured the exploit cost over ten thousand dollars, not including the inevitable doctor bills yet to come.

"Hey, Bettie, there's a Centennial Cattle Drive coming up," Vernon said as he folded over the newspaper.

Hmm, I could use a new kitchen, she thought.

Fearless Flagger

The growling of a lone aircraft echoed up the sprawling mountain draw before it popped into view, cresting a sagebrush-covered hill. Plumes of mist unfurled beneath its wings leaving behind horizontal whirlwinds. Rainbows danced off the droplets of herbicide being dispersed by the gallon in the morning sun. The ag-plane banked left to adjust its course and charged down the hill toward the silhouette of a teenage boy waving a two-foot square, red flag at the end of a short pole. He stood his ground as the plane, just three feet above the plants, snarled toward him. At what seemed like the very last moment, the aircraft lurched upward, missing the boy, leaving behind a rain of chemical that settled lazily to earth.

As the winged tractor made a hard climbing left turn, the youth lowered his flag and took off along the fence line, counting his rapid strides as he went. One... two... three... He knew he had to be at twenty before the pilot completed his final 180° turn to the right to come swooping down again. Nineteen... twenty. Just in time, he swung around and waved his flag as the airplane roared only feet above his head, then dropped down to dispense its sagebrush-killing cloud of herbicide on a new row of unsuspecting plants.

The boy watched as the plane grew smaller, dragging a misty tail behind. As it reached the top of the hill, wings glinted in the daylight indicating a slight bank to the right. A course adjustment seemed unusual, but there remained no time to think about that. One... two... three... His long slender legs carried him the next twenty paces marking the end of the upcoming swath the ag-plane would travel.

Several minutes passed before the sprayer's return, time to sit and enjoy the splendor of the mountains hiding in a blue haze off to the west. A meadowlark's song drifted over the yellow grass. A slight breeze carried a fresh mountain aroma that, for a moment, washed away the smell of 2-4D and diesel fuel still lingering in the air. Off in the distance, the low rumble of the ag-plane echoed through the hills.

Why kill the sagebrush, the boy wondered. The stony ground was obviously not fit for farming. If there were any cattle around, little evidence existed. It didn't make sense to the youth, but it didn't matter, he enjoyed being in the country, working for an aerial applicator. To his thinking, agricultural pilots were the quintessential fliers. He hoped to attain that status one day.

In the meantime, getting doused daily with chemicals and having his worn denims and beat-up jeans jacket smell to high heaven, became a badge of honor for a flagger. Living out of a small camper with no running water for bathing and nowhere to do laundry made for interesting times when the crew showed up for dinner at small-town cafes. Often their seating section would clear out as other patrons moved as far away from the agricultural aroma as possible. The teenager felt he had the greatest summer job in the world.

The boy rose to his feet as the growl of the ag-plane grew louder. A moment later it came into view as it skimmed over the top of the hill. As soon as the pilot caught sight of the red flag, he adjusted his course to the left and barreled down the hill toward it. The odd deviation once again caught the youth's attention. Something appeared wrong. Someone must be out of place.

Two local men had been hired to help with the flagging that morning because of the hilly terrain. On a flat field, there would be one flagger. Here a flagger took a position at each end with a third flagger in the middle because the pilot couldn't see from one end of the spray field to the other. In this case, the field ends were several miles apart. The two newly hired inexperienced flaggers had been given specific instructions. It became obvious to the boy that one had not followed the plan.

After the plane zoomed over the youth's head, a portable radio clipped to his belt crackled to life with the angry voice of the pilot, "What the hell are you doing? How many paces are you taking."

The young flagger unclipped the radio, held it to his cheek, and pressed the send button. "I'm taking twenty."

"Two! What are you, an idiot?" The roar of the engine in the background accentuated the pilot's anger as he circled overhead.

"No, sir. Twenty!"

"Two! Two! You've got to be kidding! Do you have any idea how much your screw-up is costing me?" The enraged voice on the radio screamed.

In total frustration at being misunderstood, the boy pushed hard on the transmit button, "No, Bill, twenty. I'm taking twenty paces."

No use. The static on the radio prevented a clear transmission and the boy's plea went unanswered. He raced his twenty paces to his next location. The aircraft roared low over his head, releasing its nasty herbicide early so it rained down on the boy. He knew it was on purpose, although he had been drenched many times before. That came with the territory.

As the plane disappeared over the hill, the stunned flagger plodded on to his next post. Confused about how the pilot could believe he would get things so wrong, particularly after all this time, he sat down to think. Each stride took approximately three feet. Twenty paces equaled sixty feet. Certain sixty feet defined the swath width, he knew he couldn't have made a mistake.

A cloud of spray created a halo around the airplane as it appeared once again over the hilltop. The boy took up his position and slowly waved his red flag back and forth. The plane grew larger as it came straight at him, gobbling up the air space between them. He remembered how he used to duck when the plane soared overhead, although it always cleared him by ten to twenty feet. He got used to the rush and now stood erect. The plane kept coming head-on. He waved his flag. With clouds of spray trailing behind, the aircraft bore down on the youth. The seconds rushed by but the airplane didn't zoom up at the last moment. Instead, it charged directly at the boy.

When he realized the airplane wasn't going to pull up there wasn't time to duck, so he simply fell over backward as the wheels of the crop sprayer raced menacingly close overhead. Had he remained standing he was sure he would have most certainly been hit. The teenager lay flat on his back, heart-thumping over the near-collision.

The crop sprayer continued south and disappeared over the hills to pick up another load of chemical, leaving a startled youth lying in the dust on his back. Picking himself up, he brushed off the dirt, and stared into the distance toward the vanishing sprayer, shaking his head in disbelief. No doubt the pilot was mad and trying to scare him, but a tragedy was barely avoided.

Turnaround for reloading the airplane usually took about twenty minutes—enough time to eat the sandwich the boy brought with him, and to relax. He found a large flat rock to stretch out on and soak in some of the morning sun. Morning chill remained in the air and the warm sun felt good. He had no way of communicating with the pilot or the other flaggers. The radio only worked line-of-sight when the airplane flew in the air above him.

He had no alternative but to wait and keep his position for when the pilot returned.

Twenty minutes passed with no sign of the airplane. Another twenty minutes went by without the familiar sound of an approaching aircraft. Minutes turned into two hours before he spotted the old, beat up, white company pickup across a gully with someone waving at him, gesturing for him to come. He quickly made a small pyramid of stones to mark his spot, grabbed his brown rucksack, and headed for the truck. The loader, a Hispanic fella who fueled the aircraft and loaded the hopper with chemicals, greeted him.

"I already got the other two guys and took 'em back to base," Jose said.

"What happened?" the boy asked. "Bill didn't come back."

"Dios Mio, he was mad when he landed. He was cursing up a mean streak, tossing things around. He grabbed the fuel hose from me and told me to back off. Said he'd do it himself. I don't think I've ever seen him so mad."

"Did he say I screwed up?" the boy asked as he climbed into the cracked and worn passenger seat.

"Si. He was especially mad at you. Said you

were costing him a bundle. Said it served him right for hiring a bambino."

"Am I in big trouble?" The boy shrunk into the seat.

"Naw. Señor Bill is the one in big trouble."

"What do you mean?"

"Uno momento, you'll see."

The dingy pickup bounced over the rocky slopes, down through a small valley, and up to the hilltop where base camp had been established. Selected because of the long flat ridge, the hilltop had enough area to land the airplane. Bill ran the pickup up and down the ridge several times to make a runway path. The tank truck and camper were parked by the few spindly pine trees at one end.

As they approached the top of the hill, the boy could see Bill and the other two flaggers sitting in lawn chairs next to the camper. The tank truck sat parked but the airplane was missing.

"Where's the airplane?" the boy asked his companion.

"Over there." The driver pointed halfway down the ridge.

There sat the airplane, one wing dragging on the ground and the other pointing toward the sky, looking like a crippled duck with a broken leg.

The teenager's eyes opened wide. "What happened?"

"You remember the red gas can we put on that big boulder in the middle of the runway? The one that Senior Bill would veer around on his takeoff run."

"Yeah."

"Well, he didn't"

"Didn't what?"

"Didn't veer around. He got so mad he forgot all about it. When he hit that thing it sent him ten feet in the air and he came down—splat."

"Man, he's gonna tear my head off, but it wasn't my fault. I was doin' right. He told me twenty paces and that's what I took."

"Aw, don't worry, man, he's cool."

The pickup pulled up to the camper and the boy cautiously approached pilot Bill.

"Hey, kid. Sorry, it took so long to pick you up." Bill greeted the boy as if nothing had happened.

The boy held out both hands in explanation, "I tried to tell you I was taking twenty paces, but the radio squelch was too noisy."

"Yeah, I know. I figured the whole thing out once I calmed down. I was the one who really screwed up. I lost my temper and ended up wrecking my plane. Stupid. Really stupid."

Bill tilted his head towards the man slouching in a lawn chair a few feet away. "Steve, here, got things wrong. He got twenty paces and sixty feet mixed up. He took sixty paces. It wasn't your fault and I want to apologize for yelling at you." The pilot stuck out his hand.

A broad smile erupted on the teenager's sunburned face. "Apology accepted. I still say this is the best summer job ever."

White Flight

Mid-December hung over the airfield in Hebron, Nebraska like a cold, grey shroud. Rapid City, South Dakota, was four hundred miles to the northwest, and I wanted to be there before sundown. Stacks of flying magazines had been read while downing a bottle of soda pop and several candy bars as I waited all morning in the small flight office for the weather to break. A glittering of snowflakes sporadically floated down from the dull luminous overcast. An occasional orange glow hinted that the sun was trying to burn a hole in the drab blanketed sky but its efforts were defeated by the thick clouds.

My newly acquired Piper Super Cub could cruise at just over one hundred miles per hour. After liberating it from its life as a crop sprayer, I was taking it home to convert it into a backcountry flyer. If I could get off by one o'clock, I could make my first stop, Rapid City, before dark.

"A low, thousand-foot ceiling all the way with possible light snow," the voice of the weatherman at the Flight Service Station predicted.

My plane had no instruments for flying in the clouds and no radio for communication. Visual Flight Rules were the only option, and that didn't look too promising.

The time of "go or no-go" was approaching rapidly. The low ceiling would not be a problem if it held. I had plenty of experience close to the ground. I could put the Cub down in a field or on a road if I had to, although the thought wasn't too appealing given the freezing temperatures.

Skud-running—flying the thin layer of clear air between the ground and a low, ragged overcast, that is what I would be doing. Young and foolish? Yes, but the decision was made.

I called the Flight Service Station back again to file a flight plan. My destination at Rapid City had a control tower. Since I had no radio, I asked the briefer to alert the tower to my estimated time of arrival of 5:00 pm. Normal procedure for non-radio airplanes was to circle outside the traffic pattern within sight of the airport until the tower operator beamed a green light from his light gun, indicating a clearance to land. I would get there at twilight and look for the signal.

With a full tank of gas and my aviation chart on my lap, I lifted off into the dreary sky and took up a heading to Rapid City. For the first hour, the long boring expanse of brown and barren Nebraska cornfields crawled by under my wings on an endless conveyor, dotted occasionally with a farmhouse or small town. I had to wonder about the people who chose that lifestyle. What kept them in this mundane, flat, and frigid country with miles between neighbors?

The bare trees and occasional frozen over ponds gave no hint that the wind was picking up from the west. Although the ride was smooth enough, the fields and country roads passed by more slowly. I took time measurements between waypoints and found my ground speed had decreased. I wasn't traveling at the 110 mph that I anticipated. The developing headwind had reduced my progress to 80 mph. The afternoon light was already beginning to fade. Luckily, the overcast remained stable above me and only a few flakes of snow struck the windshield. Rapid City was still a long way away as I flew on.

My watch read three o'clock when I reached the halfway mark on my chart. Light snow began to flash over my windshield. The fields below turned from brown to white. My ground speed remained slow as the headwind continued to restrict my forward motion like swimming upstream against the current. The ceiling ahead was dropping. Ragged grey wisps hung low beneath the overcast. I was going to miss my ETA by at least an hour. The Super

Cub droned on as my grip on the control stick grew tighter.

The sky slowly darkened and snow began falling heavier. Forward visibility was a blur of white streaks crashing headlong into the windshield at a hundred miles per hour. Looking straight down from the side windows, those same flakes fell gently to the ground to join a peaceful carpet of their relatives. How strange to be blinded looking forward, yet perfectly clear and serene looking down.

I held the compass course and followed the landmarks with my finger along the straight red line I had drawn between Hebron and Rapid City. Forty minutes to go, I estimated. The sky was now a dull grey as the light faded, but the snow added a strange iridescence as it reflected the remains of the day. The onslaught of angry flakes blocked all forward visibility. Down and behind were my only points of reference. I could see where I was, where I had been, but not where I was going.

Red and green wingtip navigation lights gave an almost festive glow to the white powder speeding past them, although I felt far from festive. This is getting serious. I had to find the Rapid City airport soon and needed some definite features on the ground to guide me. I let down to five hundred feet to better see the ground that was disappearing in the time between day and night.

There's a highway. Is it the interstate? No, the angle is wrong. Wait. It's a railroad track. Check the chart. Yes, that's what it is—it's the track that runs into Rapid City from the south. The airport is somewhere north, but there is no way to find it. I can barely see a quarter-mile ahead. If I leave the railroad track I won't know where I am. Stick with the track. Follow it into town—it eventually crosses the highway. Then I can follow the highway out to the airport.

Down to three hundred feet. Snow comes down hard as I watch the railroad tracks not far below my wheels guide me through the white curtain ahead. Slowly buildings appear, sparse at first, but more and more as the town unfolds in the small circle of vision below. Soon there are the flat roofs of commercial buildings with parking lots. The tracks lead on.

Two black ribbons, side by side, emerge from the dim haze and cut across the tracks. *The highway. That's gotta be the highway.*

I bank hard right to keep my new guide

from disappearing from view.

I scan the chart on my lap. There is barely enough light to make out the details. My finger makes an indent where the railroad tracks and highway converge and then follows the highway east. *Six miles to go. About five minutes more. I hope they can see me when I get there.*

Car lights make the highway easier to follow than the tracks. I check my watch every thirty seconds to make sure I have an accurate idea of where I am. But with the light almost gone and white all around, how will I see the airport?

The minutes tick away as the highway seems to be moving rather than the plane. The Cub feels motionless as though dangling in a white sky as the earth rotates below.

What's that? A flashing beacon. Could it be the tower? The time is right. The dark white wall of falling snow reluctantly reveals a small flash of light every few seconds as the strong blinking beam penetrates the shroud.

I hope they can see me. Stay over the highway and I will be out of the traffic pattern, although I doubt anyone is landing in this stuff.

I bank to the left and began circling, watching for the green beam that meant I had permission to land over there somewhere hidden from sight.

Wait, that beacon is wrong. It's just flashing white. It should be alternating green and white.

I edged closer to the source until it comes into view.

A water tower. It's a water tower. Where's the airport?

I roll out, pick up the highway, and head east once again.

What's that ahead? It looks like lightning flashing through the clouds. No. They're regular flashes. ALS. They're the strobe lights of the airport Approach Lighting System! They must have turned them on for me. They knew I was coming.

Although I couldn't see the airport or the runway, the glowing flashes of white drew me toward them. I knew they were located at the end of the runway and all I had to do was fly parallel to them to enter the pattern. Then I would extend beyond them and swing around, base to final approach, and the lights would guide me in. Once lined up, the three sets of bright lights at the end of the runway would tell me if I was too high, too low, or just right.

Snow was now falling from the sky in big flakes obscuring everything around. The ground below was difficult to see but I had those lights—those wonderful lights. I flew the pattern and turned to the final approach, guided by luminary angels beckoning me to safety.

Stress flowed out of my hands and my grip on the controls loosened as I glided down the path to a smooth three-point landing and rolled to a slow taxi. The runway was long and wide, made for airliners. The Cub could have landed in the length of the large painted numbers barely visible on the end of the runway. In the distance, I could see the glow of the terminal building, the beacon flashing green and white atop the tower, and the fixed base operation's sign. I turned off at the first runway exit and taxied in their direction. The runway and taxiways were white with powder as clouds of the cold stuff trailed behind the Cub. I made my way to the tie-down area, pulled into one of the open spots, and shut down the engine. Time to sit quietly, wings gently rocking in the wind, and let my nerves drain.

Reaching forward, I patted the top of the Cubs instrument panel. “Well done–well done,” I whispered. A sense of pride spread over me. Sure, it wasn’t the smartest thing to do, but I did it and I survived.

I opened the door just as the FBO attendant, wrapped in a parka and shielding his face from the blowing snow walked up.

“Where did you come from?” he said in an excited voice.

“Hebron,” I answered casually.

“No, I mean just now.”

“Hebron. I just landed.”

“No kidding! You landed in this stuff?”

He helped me tie down the Cub for the night and invited me into the flight office for a hot cup of chocolate.

“I better call the tower,” I said, brushing the snow from my shoulders. “Can I use the phone?”

“No problem.” He swung the desk phone around and pushed it toward me. “The numbers there on the bulletin board.”

“Hello, this is Piper November 85 Zulu. I called ahead for a no-radio landing clearance, and I want to close my flight plan.”

“Yes, we have your flight plan. You want to cancel it?”

“Yes, close it, I just landed.”

The voice on the other end sounded surprised. “You what? You landed here? When?”

“Yeah, a few minutes ago. Thanks for turning on the ALS lights for me. It would have been tough to find you without them.”

“No kidding. You just landed? We never even saw you. Those lights were for a Frontier flight that decided to divert to Billings because of the weather. The airport is closed.”

“Really?” Uh, oh. I landed without permission and on a closed airport. “I thought I had been cleared in. Am I in trouble?”

There was a pause on the other end of the line, but I could hear a muffled conversation going on. A few seconds later the tower operator came back on the line. “No. We’ll let this one go. We’re just glad you made it down safely.”

I thanked him for his thoughtfulness, picked up my flight bag, and turned to the FBO operator, “so, how do I get to a hotel?”

Stuck In IUSTA

I have often passed through Iusta many times over my lifetime, but my recent stay lasted longer than ever before. I suppose that has to do with my advanced age. A lot of nice people live there, some bigger than life. It is a comfortable community, well suited to someone in their twilight years. That is not to say that there are not quite a few younger people in residence. It is not an exclusive community.

I have a lot of good memories in Iusta and some not so good as well. Nostalgia seems to be a prevalent trait among those living there. The longer I stay, the more nostalgic I get. When I gather together with friends and neighbors, we enjoy sharing our pasts and relating our life experiences. I suspect often the stories are somewhat embellished by time and distance, but no one questions a good tale.

The thing is, there is no direct route to Iusta. One can't just arrive. The road there is full of twists and turns. A significant amount of travel time is required regardless of where one is coming from. The trip itself lends credence to the stories told over coffee and donuts.

I truly enjoy my visits but after a time I become restless and uneasy. The comfortable environment fades as the nostalgia begins to wear thin. I find myself repeating tales of my past that I have told too many times before. A bit of sadness creeps in as I contemplate the possibility that Iusta may become my permanent home in the not too distant future if I let it.

I have spent time in some surrounding communities that are even less attractive, so I shouldn't be too critical. There is Shuda to the west, but the people of Shuda seem unsettled and depressed. I have been tempted to get a place there, if only as a retreat. I could sit on the porch, look out at the world, and ponder all the possibilities in life that passed me by. Foresight tells me that all too soon I would fit right in—not an attractive prospect.

Now, the residents of Kuda to the east, are always bragging about their abilities. I admit I have been guilty of that same malady on occasion, but those people never seem to accomplish anything. They talk a lot. Their location has a lot of potential but no one seems to follow through with anything in Kuda.

Occasionally, I have found myself attracted to

Wooda lying to the south of Iusta. It's a community of reasonably competent and congenial people. They seem to have a comfortable life, although they often express regret in their life choices.

A part of me is attracted to Wooda. I've had a good life, a great family, interesting and challenging jobs. A visit there makes me wonder what life would have been like had I chosen a different path. I will most likely visit there from time to time, but too much water has passed under the bridge for a permanent stay.

There is another community to the north that has a preponderance of young people. Of course, individuals of all ages live there but the younger residents tend to have more energy and an upbeat attitude than others. In Gunna, most people are excited about the future. They tend to make plans and share their enthusiasm with anyone who will listen. The truth is, most of them will eventually end up in one of the surrounding communities, but a few will bust out of the norm and achieve great things. I like the energy in Gunna but I have to admit, it tires me out. I guess experience has taught me that the road out of town is most often longer and rougher than one anticipates.

At times I've visited them all, Gunna, Kuda, Shuda, and Wooda, but Iusta continues to call me back. I suppose, someday I will succumb to the inevitable when I no longer have any alternative. In the meantime, I will prod myself to stay on the road of life, creating new experiences, challenges, and accomplishments so that, when I finally get stuck in Iusta, I will have a satchel full of tales to keep myself, and my listeners entertained.

A great philosopher once said, "I yam what I yam, and that's all that I yam." I try to keep that in mind.

Wartime Christmas

The flight of lumbering B-24 Bombers growled their way through the cold night air, moonlight reflecting off their silver wings as they broke formation. One by one, they lined up on the distant runway lights, pilots concentrating on attitude, speed, and altitude with the intent of making a perfect night landing. This was the final flight for Lt. Drake and his crew, ending several months of intense training in the big four-engine bird.

Pueblo, Colorado had served as a temporary home for him and his young family while he prepared for war. Orders had been received for Topeka, Kansas where he would find out what fate had in store for him. But, tonight, he had other worries on his mind.

He had asked to see his commanding officer the day before. “Sir, I would like an emergency leave. My one-year-old daughter is very sick, and I need to take her and my wife home to Montana before we are shipped out.”

Lt. Drake’s daughter had measles. He wanted to make sure his family was taken care of before he departed for destinations unknown. “We can leave first thing the morning after my last flight, and drive to Billings. Once there, I can catch the train and be in Topeka by the 27th.”

The Commander had been sympathetic and granted a Leave of Absence with the understanding that he would be in Topeka on time.

In the darkness of early morning, the twenty-two year old, Lt. Drake loaded his wife and ailing daughter into their old '36 Chevy coupe. The trip to Billings, Montana six hundred miles away would be long.

As they passed through Denver before the city awoke, light falling snow sparkled in the headlights. Dawn broke with a heavy overcast as Cheyenne came into view.

Bundled in her mother's arms, little Lana, exhausted from her fever, rested quietly. A blessing since her crying had made sleep the night before almost impossible.

Snow became heavier as they traveled, and soon the road was white and slick. The further north they pushed, the worse it became until they were the only car on the narrow two-lane Wyoming highway. Wind whipped white barricades across their path and reduced forward visibility to a few yards.

"Hold on, Betsy," Lt. Drake called out to his wife as he struggled to regain control of the car that had lost traction on the slippery road.

The vehicle headed for the barrow pit and plowed into a snowbank in slow motion sending the white powdery stuff flying in all directions. Luckily, the car had no damage but it took a trucker with a long chain to pull the car out and get them on the road again. With little alternative, they forged ahead into the blizzard. Several more times the car lost traction and ended up off the road. Each time a helpful trucker pulled them out.

"Follow me and stay in my tracks," a grizzled face trucker said, taking pity on the serviceman and his tired family. "I'll get you there."

The big semi plowed through the winter weather all the way to Billings with a Chevy coup close in trail.

After sixteen hours of fighting the worst snowstorm of the season, the overly fatigued couple pulled into the driveway of the little white farmhouse on Washington Street at nine o'clock, Christmas Eve. The baby's fever had broken and she felt somewhat better. Grandparents took over her care while the weary travelers got a well-deserved night's sleep.

Christmas Day passed with parents, grandparents, family, and friends. Everyone knew that Lt. Drake would soon be heading off to war so the mood weighed heavy with mixed emotions. The following day amidst tearful goodbyes, he boarded a train for Topeka, Kansas.

Crossing the Midwest by rail progressed slowly but far better than battling icy roads. After a full day and night, the weary airman arrived in Topeka at 4:00 in the morning on the 27th, just in time to make reveille. An exhausted Lt. Drake fell out in formation with his fellow crew members at 5:00 a.m. to the announcement that all had been granted a ten-day leave.

Youth has its benefits, and one is stamina. The young Lieutenant repacked his suitcase and boarded the next train west, this time making a brief stop in Minneapolis to visit a brother and other family members.

Finally arriving back in Billings, he spent the evening again with Bettie and baby Lana, looking forward to a relaxing week before his assignment. The next morning, a knock came at the door.

"It's a telegram for you," Bettie called to her husband content with bouncing little Lana on his knee. "From the war department."

Lt. Drake's face dropped when he read the contents. "All leaves canceled. Return to base for overseas assignment."

After another round of tearful goodbyes from family and friends, Lt. Drake once again boarded the train to Topeka, Kansas. This time he didn't know if or when he might return. War took him halfway around the world. The farm boy from Montana found himself traveling through far off places he had barely heard of; Puerto Rico—Natal, Brazil—Dakar, Africa—Casablanca—Cairo—Karachi—Calcutta, and finally to a base in Pandaveswar, India, where he flew thirty-three missions against the Japanese in Burma and hauled gasoline and supplies into China.

On September 2nd, 1945 the Japanese signed an Instrument of Surrender aboard the USS Missouri in Tokyo Bay ending World War II. In November, Lt. Drake flew a B-24 back to the United States to be reunited with Bettie and Lana in time to celebrate a real Christmas together.

Emma's Ride

The smile on Emma's face didn't hide her nervousness. She had bravely climbed into the back seat of my Aeronca Champ, a small tube and fabric, two-place airplane born in the mid-1940s. After first meeting this lovely girl earlier in the week, I had convinced her that she needed to see the countryside from a thousand feet in the air.

"I've never been up in an airplane before," she protested. "Let alone a little one."

"You'll love it," I prompted. "I won't do anything scary, I promise."

The last thing I wanted to do was scare my newly acquired friend. It had been a while since my last romance. Female companionship came hard in this small Wyoming town. There weren't a lot of young single ladies available. I felt very fortunate to find Emma apparently available, she was quite attractive and smart.

"Here, let me fasten your seatbelt." Standing by the open door, I reached in and dug out the belts from the tight spaces on each side of the seat. Emma swept back her long blond hair as I wrapped the belt around her small waist and clicked it together on her lap. Her fresh smell was intoxicating. My pulse raced a little at being so close.

"I'm nervous," she said with a girlish giggle.

"Don't be, this will be fun," I answered in my most assuring and professional voice. "I do this every day."

The fact that I arrived as the new guy in

town, a daring crop duster, charter pilot, and flight instructor, helped make the initial desired impression. Now, I needed to reinforce that with confidence and gentle manners. What better than a smooth, uneventful airplane ride on a beautiful summer morning?

Most small airplanes from the forties don't have electric starters, and my Champ was no exception. That meant someone had to flip the propeller to get the engine started. After a thorough scan of the empty flight line with no one around, that someone would have to be me.

"See these small pedals down by your feet? Not the large ones that look like a tee, but the ones to each side." I followed her shapely legs down and pointed out the rectangular pads protruding from the floorboard. "Those are the brakes. I'm going to need you to push on them while I start the engine."

Emma's eyes grew large as she softly grabbed my shoulder. "You want me to do what?"

"It's no big deal. I just need you to hold the brakes while I start the engine," I said in a calm, reassuring voice. "It'll be fine."

Emma's smile flattened and her forehead

wrinkled. "Well, okay. If you say so."

I could tell she wasn't fully convinced but I had evidently made a good enough impression that she trusted me.

With the ignition turned off, mixture lever pulled back, and throttle closed, I pumped some fuel into the carburetor with the primer. "I'm going around to the front of the airplane to pull the propeller through a few times. The engine won't start. I'm just getting it ready, but I still want you to hold the brakes."

"Okay," she said weakly.

The fact that Emma had never been in an airplane before no doubt worked in my favor because she was probably unaware that most airplanes have electric starters. She seemed to accept this procedure as normal, although the strain in her face expressed an uncertainty about her decision to put her life in the hands of this young, daring pilot.

"Push the brakes, now," I called from my position at the front of the plane. With a firm grasp on the propeller, I pushed and pulled to rock the airplane, making sure the brakes were locked. "Good."

Rotating the propeller through four or five complete revolutions drew fuel from the carburetor into the cylinders; ready to ignite when the switch was turned on.

"You can relax for a minute," I said, as I swung in under the overhead wing strut and reached into the front cockpit. I pushed in the mixture control, cracked the throttle open a half-inch, and turned the ignition switch to both mags.

Softly touching Emma's arm, I said, "You're doing great. We'll do the same thing, only this time the engine will start."

I took up my position at the nose of the craft. "Brakes locked?"

"Yes," came a forced reply.

With a push and pull on the prop to make sure, I grabbed one blade and swung it down hard while backing away.

Tick, tick, tick, tick

The propeller rotated to a stop without the satisfying pop pop of fuel being ignited.

"Once more," I called to Emma. I could see the strain on Emma's face as she forced down on the brake pedals. She was taking her task seriously.

I stepped forward and pulled down hard.

tick, tick, tick, tick

This wasn't how it was supposed to happen;

the engine always started on the first or second try.

"Okay, hang on." I ducked under the wing and reached into the front cockpit once again. "Ignition, off—mixture back—throttle full open." I looked back at Emma.

"Is it alright?" she asked.

"Oh, yeah," I said. "Just got to clear its throat. I'll pull it through a few more times, and then we'll start over."

Back to the front, I called for brakes once more, jostled the airplane, and pulled the propeller through several revolutions.

Returning to the cockpit, I pulled the throttle back to the half-inch setting, pushed in the mixture knob, and turned on the ignition switch. "She'll go this time."

"Brakes locked?"

Once again I gave a mighty swing of the propeller.

tick, tick, tick, tick, tick

Another try.

tick, tick tick, tick

The morning sun was beginning to heat up, and I was feeling it, as I grew damp under my shirt.

"I think she's flooded. We'll have to try and

clear it again."

"Really?" Emma's voice now had the ring of concern. "We don't have to do this now. We can go flying some other time."

"Let's give it one more try. I know you will really enjoy it once we get going." I could feel Emma's confidence slipping away. I had to get her in the air. "We'll just clear its throat again. That should do it"

I reached forward, pulled back the mixture, and pushed the throttle wide open.

Returning to the front of the airplane, I called to Emma, "I'm just gonna pull it through a few more times before we start it. Brakes set?"

Emma nodded.

I pulled down on the blade.

VAROOM!

The propeller instantly jumped from my hands as the engine went to full power. In shock, I stumbled backward to get out of the way. The ignition switch, you idiot, flashed through my mind.

In a panic, Emma screamed as she grabbed for the sides of the cockpit. Her feet slipped off the brake pedals in her frantic attempt to find something solid to anchor to.

The old Champ lurched forward at me, engine roaring. Next stop would be the hangar door across from the tie-down area if I didn't stop the beast. By reflex, I managed to jump to the left, barely clearing the snarling propeller as it passed. I grabbed the wing strut as it crossed over my head and held on tight.

I could see Emma frozen with fright, helpless to do anything, and yelled, "pull the throttle back" but she was too shocked to move, even if she had known where the throttle was.

Pulling hard on the wing strut while being dragged along, I was able to get the angry airplane to turn and pivot around me. Working my way down the strut, hand over hand, I made it to the cockpit, reached in, and jerked back the throttle just as the engine died. Luckily, I had shut off the mixture so the engine had only the fuel in the carburetor bowl to feed its mad frenzy.

The airplane rolled to a stop with my heaving body hanging half out of the door, and the Champ's stunned passenger pasted hard against her seat back. Any male ego I had lie quaking at the soles of my feet. We both remained locked in that position, breathing heavily for what felt like minutes.

Finally, I slowly arose. "I think we'd better call it a day," I said without looking up.

"That's a good idea," Emma said as she slowly unbuckled her seat belt.

The ride back to town passed rather quietly.

Too embarrassed to call, I never saw Emma again.

Within six months I moved on to another job in another state.

I wonder if Emma ever got her airplane ride?

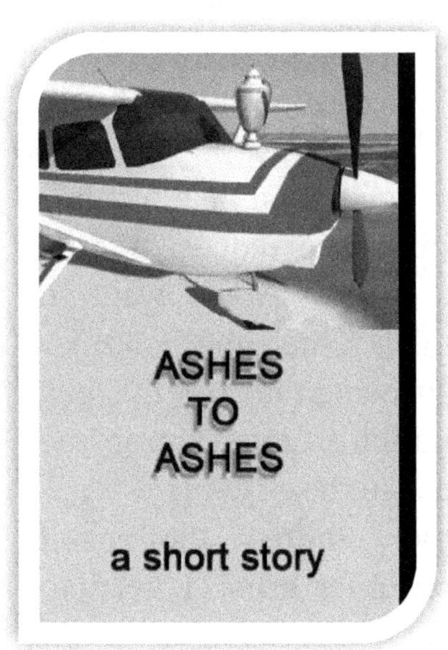

Ashes To Ashes

He walked into the flight office carrying a small cardboard box under one arm. "Your sign says, 'Air Charter.' I'd like to have someone take me up."

"I can help you," I said, as I sized up the

thirty-something, slender guy in a sports shirt and khaki pants. “Where do you want to go?”

“Do you know where the Hogsback is?”

“The Hogsback? Do you mean the ridge that runs up Mt. Helena?”

“Yeah, that’s it. I need someone to fly me over the Hogsback.”

“I can do that. Are you gonna take pictures or something?” I found the request a little unusual. Sometimes realtors would want to take aerial pictures of a neighborhood, or people wanted a sightseeing tour but this guy had a specific destination in mind up on the mountain that overlooked the city.

My new customer shifted the small cardboard box to his other arm. “I need to drop something.”

“Drop something?”

“Well, not exactly.” He placed the box on the counter. “This is my Uncle Joe’s ashes. He loved hiking up there. Before he passed away he requested his ashes be sprinkled over the area. I want to honor that request. I figured the easiest way is to drop them from an airplane.”

I heard of others doing that, although never experienced it myself. But, hey, this is business, and I could use the work. How hard could it be, fly over the mountain—open the window—dump out the ashes.

"We can do that," I answered with confidence. "When do you want to go up?"

"Now, if possible."

"Let me check the schedule." I scanned my desk-pad calendar with all its notes, circles, and doodles. I knew I had the time but I wanted to make a good impression. "Looks like we have a Cessna 172 available, and I have an opening."

"Great. I'm ready when you are."

We walked out to the Cessna, and I loosened the tie-down ropes.

"You can hop in on the right side while I do the preflight," I directed.

He slid into the seat, strapped on the seat belt, and sat the box on his lap.

After completing my check of the airplane, I stopped at his door. "This window swings open like this." I twisted the latch and pushed the window out. "I have to slow the airplane way down, so don't open the window until I tell you to."

"Okay," he replied. "I've got it."

We taxied out, took off, and climbed into

the valley. My passenger sat quietly looking out the window as we gained altitude. Soon he turned and asked, “shouldn’t we be going the other way?”

“I have to gain three-thousand feet to safely cross the mountain ridge. I’m just circling as we climb.”

“Oh.” He turned back and watched the town slowly shrink below.

As we circled, Mt. Helena rotated into view showing the long ridge that ran from its peak to the south, topped by a favorite hiking trail for locals and visitors alike. Green forest blanketed the side of the mountain overlooking the legendary gold-strike town of Helena, now Montana’s capital.

I turned the airplane to line up parallel with the ridge, pulled back the power, and dropped the flaps. My passenger had opened his cardboard box and extracted a stainless steel urn that I assumed contained Uncle Joe’s ashes.

Once the plane was slow enough, I instructed, “you can open your window now.”

The young man twisted the latch and pushed open the window. Seventy miles-per-hour wind overpowered the growl of the engine. He lifted the lid from the urn and tipped the container up to the window and over.

I believe it was at that moment that Uncle Joe had a change of heart and decided he didn't really want to fall the five-hundred feet to the forest trail below. In fact, he decided not to leave the airplane at all and made an abrupt one-eighty to join us back in the cockpit. My stunned passenger dropped the urn to the floor, grabbed the window, and slammed it shut, but it was too late. We became intimately acquainted with Uncle Joe as his ashes swirled around, coating us with a light grey powder from head to foot. I sputtered and sneezed as Uncle Joe invaded my eyes, ears, nose, and mouth.

At times like this, one really wonders about the wisdom of making uninformed decisions.

I looked over at my client, his eyes the size of saucers, he swatted at ash like it was a swarm of bees.

Moments later, as the ash settled, we sat motionless in the realization of what had just happened. Uncle Joe now coated the inside of my airplane instead of his final resting place among the serene pines below.

I heard myself leak my thought out loud, "I hope he likes to travel."

Uncle Joe's nephew turned toward me, and our eyes met. His face was blank and white with ash. I held my breath, not knowing what else to say. We stared for a moment, and then he burst out in a huge guffaw.

Wiping his face, he roared over the engine, "leave it to Uncle Joe to get the last laugh."

Man, I felt relieved to hear that.

We flew back to the airport and taxied up to the maintenance hangar. Luckily, no one was around. I wheeled the shop-vac up to the plane to rescue Uncle Joe from the indecency of his predicament.

"Should I put a new bag in the vacuum, first?" I asked. After all, that was the least I could do. It seemed sacrilegious to suck him in to spend eternity with all the dirt and grime from the hangar floor.

"Not a bad idea," my client said with a smile.

We took turns relieving Uncle Joe from our clothes and then from the cockpit of the airplane. A few candy wrappers, dead flies, and peanut shells joined him in the bag.

When we had reached all the corners and crevasses possible, I pulled the bag from the shop-vac and handed it to his nephew. “I think we got most of him.”

“Thanks,” he said. “I’m going to hike up the Hogsback tomorrow and empty it. No use telling the family what happened.”

I heartedly agreed and sent my not-so-satisfied client on his way—no charge, thank you.

After that, every time I flew that old Cessna, I swear I could hear muffled laughter under the sound of the engine . . .

“Uncle Joe?”

Tractor Parts

“I want you to take the Super Cub, and deliver some tractor parts to a farm down by Burlington.” Bill pulled aviation sectional and topographical charts from the rack of narrow shelves hanging on the wall behind the counter.

Super Cub? I love flying the Cub! Any day I can fly that airplane is a good day.

With its oversized balloon tires, seaplane propeller, and one hundred and eighty horses up front, the Super Cub is the ultimate back-country flier.

"They had a tractor break down in the field. It would take them a full day to drive up here and back. You can be down there in twenty minutes." Bill's slender frame bent over his desk as he spread out the maps. In his early thirties, he had flown tankers for the firebombing outfit, Hawkins and Powers, until he got assigned to manage their fixed-base operation here. With a strong finger, he drew a line extending south of the airport, over the town of Powell, across a long stretch of Wyoming desolation, to the Greybull River Valley.

"I see what you mean," I agreed as I studied the chart. No direct route existed across the barren landscape between the two patches of green. Parts of Wyoming are like that—miles and miles of rugged sunburnt hills, brown grass, grey dirt, and sagebrush. Everywhere, sagebrush. Occasional rivers and streams of muddy brown water struggle their way through the parched earth, often to be absorbed into a trickle or a ghost-like river of dust. What a great place for an airplane that can sail over the rugged terrain and land almost anywhere.

"The parts should be here soon. Get the plane ready."

"How will I know the place? Where should I land?"

Bill focused in on the topographical map. "See this reservoir here along the river?" His finger traced the blue line to the east of the ragged body of water that served to capture snow runoff and spring rains. "The farm sits on this bend. It's the only farm on the south side of the river in that area. Take up a heading of one hundred and fifty degrees when you leave. That should put you pretty close to the farm."

"And landing?"

"The guy said you could land on the gravel road in front of the house or in the field across the road. You shouldn't have a problem."

I folded up the topo and sectional charts, and headed out to the Super Cub tied down on the flight line, a fine example of the quintessential classic airplane. Born from the Piper J-3 that trained thousands of pilots during World War II, the airframe design had been beefed up over the years, more power added, and improvements made, resulting in the ultimate bush plane used from Alaska to Africa. The "Piper Cub" name became to aircraft what "Kleenex" is to tissue paper.

All white except for the thin red stripe down its side and Nike -like swoosh emblem on its tail, the bird looked proud sitting in the morning sun. It reminded me of the sure-footed mountain goat ram I spotted standing on a rocky outcropping the other day while flying a Fish and Game warden in search of an elk herd. With the Rocky Mountains a thirty-minute flight to the west, the Pryor Mountains to the north, and the Big Horn Mountains to the east, the planned flight across a rough and barren no-man's land to the south exemplified the stark contrasts of Wyoming's geography.

As I finished my pre-flight inspection, a pickup truck pulled in. The driver emerged dressed in a blue work shirt bearing the emblem of the tractor supply house. He handed me a small cardboard box with a label addressed to the farmer.

"Is that all of the parts?" I asked, taking the box that couldn't have weighed over a pound. "I figured I would be hauling something big and heavy."

"Yep, that's all, but the tractor won't run without it."

I put the package in the baggage compartment behind the rear seat and untied the plane. There is an art to entering a Super Cub, letting people know the pilot is a pro. I backed up to the door, reached over my head, grabbed the crossbars, and lifted myself onto the lower door frame. One more heft on the bars and I swung my legs into the cockpit followed by my rear into the seat.

Takeoff in the Cub evokes excitement in me every time. As I fed in the power it seemed to simply levitate into the air as though it couldn't wait to fly. As many times as I left the earth in this manner, the experience never got old.

Dry bluffs of Polecat Bench gave way to green fertile farmland squeezed into the Shoshone River Valley, bordered on all sides by rough brown hills. The small town of Powell slipped under my wings. To the south, the dry rugged hills with draws and gullies cut deep into their slopes looked like they were trying to hold back the parched earth beyond.

Water turned dirty brown from the escaping earth, filled the crooked river below as it meandered its way through the valley, providing lifeblood to green fields that looked out of place. A few minutes into the flight the green abruptly ended in stark contrast to the walled fortress of the sagebrush empire.

The next twenty miles I flew only a couple hundred feet above the ground where I spotted a coyote scampering for cover. A small band of antelope scattered, frightened by my noisy bird. This is their country. It belongs to the rattlesnakes, jackrabbits, and the other dry land critters. Man has no desire to claim it, although I love it, viewed from my aerial throne. Looking down, I watched my shadow race effortlessly over the ground, climbing hills, charging down washes, and up vertical bluffs.

Just as abruptly as they started, the desert hills dropped into the narrow Greybull River Valley. My compass has guided me faithfully. I can see the reservoir off to my right with its liquid-mud fingers extending into the barren hills on the south side of the valley. My eyes follow the river eastward to the bend that matches the blue line on the map on my lap. That's gotta be the place. I scan the map and then the valley below, looking for confirming landmarks. Yep, that's it.

There was, indeed, a stretch of straight gravel road in front of the farmhouse. No one mentioned the telephone poles, power poles, and fence posts on either side. I lined the Cub up to make a low pass over the road. Hmm, the road is about thirty feet wide with about ten feet on each side before the fence and poles. My wingspan is thirty-five wide. Sure doesn't leave much room for error. The spacing might have been greater, but from my vantage point, I could imagine clipping a wing and finding myself in an intimate relationship with an oil-impregnated post.

Not possible. Next.

Easing the throttle forward, I left the waiting spider web behind. A steep bank to the right gave me a look at the field beside the road. I hoped for a new growth of alfalfa or cut wheat, but the neat rows of green plants suggested otherwise. As I swung in over the field, sun reflected off rivulets of water between the rows as though narrow mirrors had been laid end-to-end separating the potato, sugar beet, or cabbage plants. I didn't know what the little green monsters were, but they were conspiring with the water to grab my wheels and flip my steed on its nose if I dare touch down.

No road, no field to land on. The river hemmed in the farm on the north and the bleached brown hills rose sharply from the field to the south.

There's got to be someplace I can put this puppy down. I can't go back. The farmer would be upset and Bill would probably hit the ceiling—no doubt he would find a place if he were here.

With the door open for a better view below, I climbed up a few hundred feet to get a lay of the land. Things looked pretty bleak but then I spotted a service trail on the far side of the field up against the steep bluffs. The two-track dirt road made by tractors and trucks skirted the edge of the field. It meandered over the base of the hills, through gullies and washes. There appeared to be one fairly straight flat stretch.

That might do ... if it's long enough and not too rough.

I circled the field and dropped down to

about fifty feet as I floated by the possible landing site, door open and head in the wind to get a good look. An old barbed wire fence with a wire gate sagged menacingly at one end of the straight section. The road had ruts and humps, being dirt tramped down by farm vehicles. About five hundred feet down the trail from the fence the road crossed a wash where occasional rain ate away at the bare soil.

I'd have to set down just after the gate and be stopped before the wash … a heck of a challenge. It's a long walk to the farmhouse too.

Every pilot secretly thinks he's exceptional, particularly Cub pilots. I was a card-carrying member of that club. If I could stick this landing, think of the bragging rights. One more pass just to make sure. I pulled up for another circuit around the field and came in low and slow. I carefully studied the two-track trail.

Yep, it looks doable.

Up and around again, this time I lined up with the road, extended the flaps and pulled the engine back to idle. The airplane settled toward the sagging gate.

Gotta clear it by only a couple of feet if I'm

going to touch down soon enough.

The gate sailed under my wheels as I flared for the landing.

Too fast. I'm floating too far.

I gunned the engine and aborted the landing. The gravel gully flashed by.

I would've hit that for sure! Gotta be slower.

As I climbed for another circuit of the field, I spotted a young teen on a motor scooter leaving a trail of dust as he raced up the dirt road on the other side toward my landing spot. He waved as he rode. I waved back through my open door.

At least I won't have to walk to the farmhouse.

I lined up on the road once again.

Slow it down ... don't stall this puppy ... clear the gate ... good ... good.

The timing and speed were right. The airplane plopped down onto the dirt on its huge-cartoon sized tires. Like the mountain goat, the machine bounced along the rutted track as I pushed hard on the brakes, working the rudder pedals to keep the right end pointed forward. In seconds, the Cub skidded to a stop.

Room to spare, I thought as I sat for a

moment relishing in the pride of a great achievement.

After shutting down, I swung my legs out the door and dismounted with all the flair of a cavalry major who had just won a great battle. The teen motored toward me on his scooter.

He's gotta be impressed! That was a great landing.

I flashed my biggest professional smile as the boy parked his motorbike and strolled over.

Dressed in farmer overalls, a ball cap covering his crew cut, and wide-eyed with awe he called out as he walked, "Boy, I sure didn't think you would land that thing here."

Yep, he's impressed alright. "Yeah, it was a challenge," I called out from my puffed-up chest. "I can put this Cub down just about anyplace."

"Just wondering why you didn't land at the BLM (Bureau of Land Management) airstrip over there?" He pointed back over his shoulder toward the hilltop.

"I ... the what?"

"Ya know, the dirt runway the rangers use up there. That's where I was waiting for ya."

My 'major' status suddenly shrunk to 'buck private.' *A strip ... up there? And I didn't see it? Uh ... oh ... think fast you idiot.* "I just like the practice," I lied.

With a quick turn, so the kid couldn't see the red flush oozing into my face, I reached into the baggage compartment, grabbed the precious cargo, and handed him the box. "Here ya go, special delivery."

"Thanks, Dad really needs this. I gotta get it out to him right away but I wanna stay and see how you take off."

"Right. Okay then."

Back in the Cub, I fired up, swung the tail around, and taxied back to the gate, wings rocking wildly in the ruts and dust clouds swirling behind the spinning prop. I pivoted around as close to the gate as I could to get all the takeoff room possible.

Make this look good.

Holding the brakes, I pushed the throttle full forward until the engine was wailing away. Brakes off, the Cub charged toward the gully wash, slowly picking up speed. The tail lifted as the plane hopped over the rough road like a jackrabbit trying to fly. One last hop just before reaching the washed-out ravine and I was in the air. I returned the waving boy's salute as I passed and headed north.

My takeoff didn't have the desired effect on my deflated ego as I had hoped. I twisted around to look back over the tail and spotted the fifteen hundred-foot grass landing strip on top of the hill. *Dumb ... really dumb.*

The flight north passed quickly. The barren hills slipped by, barely noticed, as I slinked home. After an uneventful landing back at Powell, I tied the plane down and walked slowly to the small operations building where Bill waited.

"How'd it go?" he asked from his cluttered desk. "Any problems?"

"Piece of cake," I muttered.

Stiff Company

A long black hearse pulled through the gate in the chain-link fence surrounding the airport.

Here comes my passenger, I thought as the ominous vehicle made its way to where I had parked. *This is really weird.*

I hadn't been on the job long and now on my first actual charter flight in the new Model A36 Bonanza. The sleek six-passenger airplane could cruise around two hundred miles per hour—faster than anything I had flown before. Boss-man, Dan, had checked me out in the plane a few days earlier. To say I was a green pilot was an understatement.

"I've got a job for you," Dan had said earlier that morning. "Take the Bonanza and run down to Casper. You'll pick up a corpse and bring it back here."

I gulped, "A corpse?"

"Yeah. You know. A dead person." Dan shuffled through some papers on his desk, business-like, acting nonchalant but I caught a glimpse of a momentary smile as he turned away.

Okay, he's toying with me cause I'm the new guy. "You're putting me on. You couldn't get a coffin through the door."

"No, I'm not. And there's no coffin. We get these calls pretty regularly. I fly 'em a couple times a month."

"Really? Why fly dead people?"

"Who knows? Some guy dies in Casper and the family wants him here pronto for the funeral before he spoils."

"How do you get them in the airplane? Do you sit them up in the seat?" I tried to imagine wrestling this dead body into the airplane and strapping it into the seat beside me.

Dan chuckled at my naive question without glancing up. "No. The right front seat back folds down and they lay the body on a stretcher over the seat. It's in a body bag."

I had seen body bags in the military—dozens of them lined up on the tarmac ready to load into a transport. Like long black garbage bags with a zipper down the center, the lumps and bumps only hinted at the contents inside. *I can deal with that.*

Upon arrival in Casper, a curtained limo pulled up beside my wing and two suited men stepped out. As I climbed from the cockpit, the driver waved. I gave a weak wave back to acknowledge that I was, indeed, the person they were to meet. The two men walked around to the back of the hearse, swung the tailgate open, and slid a stretcher out. A wheeled frame sprung out below the stretcher, allowing them to roll their cargo over to the wing-walk of my plane.

You've got to be kidding. It's not a black

bag!

A middle-aged man, arms crossed, dressed in a grey suit and striped burgundy tie lay motionless on the gurney shrouded in a clear plastic bag. I couldn't help staring at my passenger as I dismounted from the wing. The two attendants went about their job of getting the gentleman ready to load as though they did this every day-—and they probably did.

The Bonanza has a wide access door to the four rear seats. It is actually two doors that open like a barn so passengers can easily get in. A second door over the wing near the front of the aircraft provides access for the pilot and one additional passenger. With that passenger seat folded down, the two suited body handlers carefully slid my prone cargo through the rear doors and into place inside the airplane. After strapping the stretcher and its lifeless burden down, I signed the appropriate paper handed to me on a clipboard, took my copy, and bid the limousine drivers farewell. The body now in my care.

For some unknown reason, the Bonanza has only one forward door for the pilot and front passenger and it is on the right-hand side of the airplane. The pilot has to climb past the passenger seat to get to his command center. In this case, the passenger seat contained the headrest for a very dead person. I carefully scooted across just inches above the nose of my deceased companion. As I plopped down into my seat, the dead man's head was directly at my right side. I felt like he could open his eyes at any moment and stare directly up my nose.

Be cool. He's a stiff. He's a gonner. He's not alive. Just concentrate on flying and getting this guy back home.

I fired up the Bonanza, called the tower, and taxied out for takeoff. With all the gauges in the green and a clearance from the controller, I firewalled the throttle and lifted off. I tried to ignore the stone-cold face beside me as the airplane climbed out to the north. My route took me over the southern end of the Bighorn Mountains. Casper lies at fifty-five hundred feet in elevation. I figured I would climb to ten thousand feet to clear the mountains as I vectored into Worland. From there it was a straight shot on to Powell.

The smooth morning air turned to chop. The airplane felt like a roadster speeding down a gravel road with occasional potholes.

Climbing for altitude, the air smoothed out somewhat as we passed through nine thousand feet.

"Uhhhhhhhhhhhhh." A guttural sound filled the cockpit.

"What the heck was THAT?" I blurted out uncontrollably.

"Uhhhhhhhhhhh."

My heart skipped a beat as I looked down at my passenger to see his mouth partially open and the clear plastic shroud rippling from his breath as he moaned.

He's alive! ... Is he alive? ... What's going on? ... What should I do?

"Uhhhhhhhhhh."

I instinctively pushed the control wheel forward and leveled off at ten thousand feet. The stiff lay quietly at my side. As I stared at him, waiting for the next groan, I could detect no motion, no twitching in his face, and no movement in his chest. The eerie moaning had ceased.

Did he come alive for only a couple of minutes and then die again?

My heart beat hard against my chest as I flew on toward home, concentrating on making my course the shortest distance between two points. The dead man made no more sounds. He lay there, cold and motionless. I imaged his eyes popping open as he struggled to sit up, startled by his surroundings.

Good thing he's strapped down tight.

The miles passed under my wings in slow motion. Two hundred miles per hour felt like crawling. Slowly the airplane clawed its way home.

I radioed ahead on the Unicom, "Dan, I'm fifteen minutes out. Is there someone there to collect the body?"

I had all I could take of zombie bodies and wanted to be rid of my passenger as quickly as possible.

"Roger. An ambulance is already here," Dan replied in his normal monotone voice.

Once on the ground, I let the medics handle the body while I made my way to the flight office. I tried to hide my nervousness.

"So, how'd it go?" Dan asked.

"You know," I said in a hushed voice even though there was no one else around, "I think that guy was still alive when they loaded him in."

Dan looked at me with a stone face. "Yeah?

What makes you think so?"

"He started groaning after I took off."

"Really?"

"Yeah. Several times!"

Dan's face started to crack. "You really think he was alive? Maybe we ought to tell those medics."

He couldn't hold it any longer. With one large guffaw, he burst out laughing. "Ha, ha, ha, ha ... gotcha. Boy, you should see your face."

"What are you laughing at? Really, he was groaning."

"Sure he was. They all do that."

"They what?"

"Yeah. When you take 'em to altitude the pressure difference pushes the trapped air out of their lungs. Sometimes they even fart."

"No kidding?"

"No kidding. A lot of the times you can barely hear it, but you must have got a real groaner."

I stood there, not knowing whether to laugh or slink away in shame. I decided to laugh. Then I saw Jerry, the other new pilot walking toward the office. Hmm, no use keeping all this fun to myself. "Hey, Dan."

"Yeah?" Dan said as his laughter subsided.

“Send Jerry on the next pickup. He needs a little excitement in his life too.”

Nick Of Time

"Prescott radio, Grumman American five-eight Lima, DF check, one—two—three—four ...." We departed the Prescott, Arizona airport fifteen minutes earlier after a stop and go, and were headed for Flagstaff. The route took us over the Chino mountain range. Flight Service at Prescott, calibrating its Direction Finding equipment, requested I transmit every five minutes en route.

Rick, my student, held a relaxed grip on the controls and a finger on the sectional chart, as he checked our position. I watched the semi-arid valley floor spotted with sagebrush pass under my wing. Small settlements lay scattered over the dry landscape trying to force a reluctant desert to bloom, obviously with little success. The drab flatness soon gave way to rapidly rising terrain where small bushes seemed to grow taller and turn into scrub pine trees. Trees thickened with altitude and bunched into the rugged contours of the mountains. Once sufficiently high enough to escape the dry desert below, they gathered into forests to crown the peaks with dark green.

The American 1A trainer climbed slowly in the heat.

"Let's stay a thousand feet above the ground," I instructed as we headed for a mountain pass that would take us to the eastern slope.

Leaving the flatlands behind, anxious minutes slowly passed when a glide back to either side of the mountain range was not possible.

"Yeah, there's no place to land up here," Rick said studying the ragged tree-covered draws and crags that extended in all directions. His hand tightened on the control wheel, his knuckles showing a faint white tint.

Not fond of the trainer, I often said it flew like an ironing board with a manhole cover tied to it. The bubble-topped cockpit sat over a pair of stubby little wings. We couldn't hide from the blazing sun, and the air vents with a weak stream of hot Arizona air offered little relief. At least we encountered slightly cooler at altitude.

The airplane had what I called, "training flaps." I could never quite understand why they were added as part of the design. They did little to slow the airplane on landing or add lift.

Bang!

Without warning, violent shaking engulfed the whole aircraft. The instrument panel blurred. The convulsing engine felt like it would rip itself right out of the cowling.

"I got it!" I yelled, as my hands swept across the controls. "Mixture–rich, throttle back, carb heat on, fuel valve on both, nose down, watch the airspeed."

My emergency training took over before I could think. By the time I got to the fuel gauges, my brain caught up with my instinct.

Broken prop!

I flashed back to a couple of hours earlier at the Sedona airport when, during preflight, I found a fairly deep nick in the propeller. I asked the mechanic to dress it out. He came with a course round file and filed it down, leaving some pronounced marks. When I suggested that the marks should be burnished smooth, he said, "Aw, it will be fine. I have done dozens of these."

Obviously, not "fine," because now about twelve inches of the prop had departed and the unbalanced propeller was about to disassemble the airplane, mid-air. My automatic reflex to pull back the throttle slowed the prop and kept the engine in place, but we were now a glider—a very poor glider.

Rick sat frozen, one hand on the center console and the other with a crumpled sectional chart clenched tightly in his fist.

"Are we going down?" he mouthed the words over the unexpected silence.

"Yep." I tried to answer calmly. "Look for a place to land."

"Yeah—right." Rick's eyes bounced over the crags and crannies below.

We were still on the FSS frequency, so I keyed the mic. "Mayday, mayday, November niner six five eight Lima, engine failure."

I said engine failure because it seemed a whole lot shorter than to explain a prop separation.

FSS came back almost immediately, "Five eight Lima, we have your position approximately forty miles northwest on a heading of zero-three-zero, please confirm."

Thank goodness for that DF test. DF could tell which radial we were on, and the timed transmission along with reported airspeed gave FSS a pretty good idea of where we were.

From the moment of the bang, I had been scanning the ground for a place to land. What I saw were timber-covered mountainsides and deep gorges. Nothing resembling a flat open area to land an airplane lay below.

"Stay calm and fly the airplane," the FSS station said. "There are plenty of roads out there. Pick out a good one and set her down."

Plenty of roads? Where did he think we

were? We passed all the roads when we left the flats!

The little trainer lost altitude fast, with nothing but steep mountains and tall trees below.

"There's a logging trail—I see a logging trail snaking between the timber along the mountain slope over there," I pointed while speaking into the mic and to Rick at the same time.

I didn't want to let on that we had only one option, to line up with the trail, sink into the gap, let the trees take off the wings, and hope the fuselage stayed on the track between the tall timbers. With trees growing larger and beginning to dominate the windshield, Rick sat silently watching in disbelief

I set up my approach, lined up with the trail, and bled off airspeed, trying to hold the little trainer in the air as long as possible.

Don't stall this puppy. Keep her straight. Easy does it.

We sank rapidly toward the treetops and the slender ribbon of dirt road darting in and out of the shadows. As the tangle of green fingers reached up to snare us, a small clearing appeared on the other side of the trees and to the left. The tiny meadow had a significant slope to it, but a better choice than going into the forest. I pulled on full flaps to convert the last of our airspeed into added lift. The subtle effect boosted the rapidly descending airplane enough to make it over the tops of the spires with only inches to spare.

Once clear of the green giants, I crammed down on the left rudder, turned the control wheel hard right, and pushed forward, for a steep slip, down into the clearing.

“Hold on, this could get rough!” I blurted out.

Rick had hardly moved until that point but shot his hands forward and braced against the instrument panel.

A quick flair at the last second put us on the ground hard, heading downhill toward the stand of trees that ringed the meadow. The plane hit a small mogul and catapulted back into the air, coming down a second time with a thud. I thrust down again on the left rudder and brake, making a bouncing arc with trees flashing by our wingtip. The plane shuddered and shook as it stumbled over the tall grass and wildflowers. We slid to stop just feet from disaster; the fiberglass gear legs had held up to the beating.

In the next moment, all turned strangely quiet. I rolled back the canopy and heard birds chirping and the wind gently blowing through the pines. I inhaled a large breath of clean mountain air. A surreal calm enveloped us.

I don't know how long we sat there in disbelief of our good fortune. Time had lost its meaning. We relished the peacefulness of the mountain scene, and then Rick and I looked at each other and broke out in uncontrollable laughter.

The adrenaline drained from my brain and I keyed the mic, "Flight service, five eight Lima is on safely the ground."

The next few minutes filled with conversations with the Flight Service Station making sure that we were okay and not in shock with serious injuries.

"Are you sure you are all right?" the agent asked. "Look around. Is there any blood? Do you feel any pain? Check each other out. Are you out of the plane? Can you smell gas?"

It took some doing to convince them we were fine. In fact, we were sitting on the wing enjoying the peace and quiet.

A Bonanza pilot heard our mayday call and

flew overhead. He radioed back to Flight Service and informed them he had found us. Then, he called down to us over the radio, "How the heck did you ever get that plane into that tiny space?"

"Just lucky I guess," I answered casually, as though it were all in a day's work.

Later, we were picked up by a forest service Bell 47 helicopter. As we lifted off, we looked down at a postage-stamp-size meadow with a small white airplane at its edge in the vast timber forest. Wheel tracks in the deep grass made a sweeping turn around the perimeter in an almost complete half-circle, without touching a tree.

During the whole episode, Rick said he wasn't scared until just before touchdown when I barked, "Hold on, this could get rough."

Who had time to be scared?

Snap Rolls To Burger

Walk into the Burger King at the Sun Airpark in Scottsdale, Arizona, and you might be surprised to see a small red, white, and blue biplane hanging from the ceiling. I was astonished to learn an airplane I had owned and restored in the early '90s had been retired to a small niche in the ceiling of a burger joint. I wrote the following story in 1995 after completing the restoration of Pitts Special N20DS.

[June 1993] The handbill read, "WANTED... PITTS SPECIAL.... Middle-aged man needs Pitts Special to get through mid-life crisis... need aircraft for under $15,000."

A large, side view drawing of a Pitts S1C occupied the middle of the page so no one would mistake what I searched for. I chose hot pink paper to make sure it would catch attention. The field had been narrowed down to a Pitts after several years of pondering over the right airplane for me. I knew I wanted to fly aerobatics again and the little Pitts biplane fit the bill according to my new friends in the International Aerobatic Club.

Back in the '70s, which seems like another life, I owned an aerobatic flight school complete with Citabrias, Decathlons, and a Stearman. Located on a grass strip in California with biplanes, antiques, and warbirds, there was nary a nose gear in sight—the closest thing to heaven a "seat-of-the-pants" pilot could find. The experience spoiled me for straight and level. Chugging along, wings level, checking out the neighbor's back yard just didn't hold a thrill anymore unless I could see them cutting their grass looking up through my Decathlon's greenhouse window. That took place close to twenty years ago. The 'Great Recession' of the '70s and life's responsibilities charted a new course for this would be air jockey after trying to hang on to an aviation career with my fingernails. Oh, I have been able to stay on the fringe of my first love over the years. I have even owned a few airplanes, the last being a collection of miscellaneous, pseudo-Piper parts loosely herded together to resemble a Piper Cub. A purchase made strictly out of emotion, the right price, and I wanted a Cub. When I got the airplane home and looked under its' skin, things were not what they appeared to be. Fortunately, it got shipped somewhere overseas where it can live out its life of deception with no one being the wiser.

Two years ago I got wind of a Judges School that the IAC (International Aerobatic Club) had scheduled at the local airport here in Buffalo, Minnesota. What luck! Even if I couldn't afford an aerobatic airplane, at least I could be around them. I decided to attend even though I knew very little about IAC or what they did. Herb Hodge flew his miniature toy biplane through all the maneuvers over the chalkboard box as he walked a classroom full of aerobatic enthusiasts through the ins and outs of a contest. I had great experience and got to talk flying with other people, good people, that liked to turn airplanes upside down, too. The next thing I knew I had become a member of IAC Chapter 78.

Completely hooked, my search ensued for a steed that would carry me into the competition arena. Well, maybe a pony to start, although I didn't have thirty or forty or fifty thousand to spend. The Cub sale had left me with fifteen thousand to invest in a new toy [Remember, this is 1995]. I started looking at kit planes and plans. It didn't look as though anything came even close to my price range. I talked about planes like the Clipped Wing Cub, Citabria, Rans Sakota, RV-3 or 4, Baby Lakes, Smith Mini-Planes, and so on, dreaming of the day I would scribe those perfect figures in the sky.

I met Phil Schacht early on in Chapter 78. Phil flew a Pitts S1S, and he took an interest in me right away. He kept nudging me towards a Pitts Special, and I thought it would be great but who was going to donate the “dinero” to cover the cost. Then came my first contest at Albert Lea, Minnesota. After seeing those stubby little biplanes lined up side by side with their chests puffed out, each one waiting its’ turn to growl through a sequence, I knew I had to have one. Advice flowed freely. Just mention I wanted a Pitts and everyone had an opinion of model, engine, and accessories. I came away with two things from that first contest. One, it might be possible to find an old flat-wing, two-aileron S1C suitable for competition that would fit my pocketbook. Second, they were a great bunch of people. It didn’t matter that I didn’t have an airplane or any competition experience, from the basic pilots to the unlimited, they all were willing to share their time and experience with me. That is a rare find in today’s world.

With the resolve of locating a Pitts, I scoured the usual sources like Trade-A-Plane and General Aviation News & Flyer. I made a few trips to look at low-priced S1C models only to discover how deceiving photographs can be. Phil said he had looked at close to a dozen before he found his, and he had a whole lot more money to spend. I began to get discouraged. The Oshkosh Fly In was coming up and I figured it would be a shopping mall of aircraft. Surely I could find my dream airplane there. That is when I created the hot pink poster with a plan to tack it up all over Oshkosh and watch as the Pitts leads poured in. I also mailed fifty of them to FBOs within a three-state area asking the recipients to post them on the bulletin boards.

Oshkosh came and went and there wasn't a Pitts S1C to be found except for a plans-built project about 60% complete. Looking back on it now, it may have been a good deal but I wasn't sure I wanted to do that last 40% of the work that often takes 90% of the time. I didn't even get one response from my mailing. I resigned myself to a few more years of building my savings. Unfortunately, it seemed that airplane prices always rose faster than my savings.

Several months later, after the poster passed into history, I got a call out of the blue. "Saw your poster on our bulletin board." the voice said. "I know of a guy who has one in his hanger that he hasn't flown for twenty years.

He says he is ready to part with it; could be just what you're looking for."

A few days later I parked in front of a hangar at Anoka County Airport waiting for Otis to show up and give me a peek at his creation. He had built it with the help of some experienced Pitts builders and completed it in 1973. It had been test-flown once by an experienced pilot. It seems Otis flew the second time and ground looped it. From what I hear, it is a familiar story among new Pitts owners. At any rate, the experience frightened him enough that the plane went back in the hanger and only came out for engine run-ups over the next twenty-one years.

A big white station wagon pulled up and a short stocky guy with a friendly face climbed out to greet me. His flight jacket and cap had all the appropriate emblems, patches, and pins from fly-ins and aviation organizations. He opened his big new hangar door to reveal boats, trailers, and parts from all kinds of things including several airplane and helicopter projects. Right in front sat his pride and joy, N20DS, trying hard to look good after twenty years of dust, fading, and neglect. As I looked her over, Otis filled the air with events and people in the aerobatic world that he had known through the years. He hung with the local aerobatic crowd and had built the Pitts to compete. Unfortunately, that never came to pass but it didn't seem to dampen his enthusiasm for the sport. He had saved the plane for his son but kids have a way of choosing their own passions. His boy never developed an interest, so now the time had come to sell.

In my earlier life, I attended A&P school and, with my natural attraction to tube and rag airplanes, got involved in several rebuild projects. Now, I tried to summon up some of that ancient knowledge to evaluate this dust-encrusted airplane. I hadn't done a very good job of sizing up the Cub when I bought it, and I didn't want to make the same mistake again. The Pitts definitely needed some work. The engine had less than three hours since new but twenty-one years of sitting. Surface corrosion scarred many of the visible parts and the bottom cowling went missing. As I poked my flashlight down the fuselage, I happily found it looked as good as a three-hour-old airplane should look. The welds appeared professional and straight. In general, the airplane looked pretty sound. It needed a paint job and the engine would have to be checked out, but it had possibilities.

Phil had offered his services to inspect any airplane I might find but unavailable. The next weekend Dave Rhudrud, another Pitts owner, and Tom Tschida, Phil's mechanic, flew over in Dave's Bonanza to take a "look-see" and keep me thinking straight.

"Well, it wasn't built to be a showpiece," Tom's commented.

I had to admit it appeared kind of rough.

"That pressure carburetor needs to be tested, the diaphragms are probably rotted. An engine sitting that long is probably full of rust. Have you looked into the engine with a borescope?"

Actually, I used "hope" instead of "scope"; as in, I hope it's okay. They weren't making this easy. I wanted them to show up and say, "Great buy, take it home!" Instead, I got a bunch of caution flags.

I returned one more time without an airplane, torn between walking away or jumping in. Making a commitment to buy an airplane is hard enough. Throw in a questionable history, possible deterioration, and an unknown amount of work and it would be easier to drop all my hard-earned cash at the horse races… with better odds.

Sometimes I get this nagging little voice deep down inside which keeps saying, "Go for it! Go for it!" It may not be the most logical way of making a decision but it often turns out to be right. I think our brains take in and process information back in some deep crevice of our cerebrum that is far more efficient than our conscious thinking ability. At any rate, I went for it, holding my breath all the way.

A good friend and Clip Wing Cub owner, Dick Weber, helped me remove the wings from N20DS, and trailer it the sixty miles back to my little workshop. I don't know how Otis felt about seeing a stranger drive off with his child but I know I would have had to grab my sunglasses to cover my watery eyes. Once in my shop, I started inspecting every inch of my new toy. October had ended, and I figured I would have her in the air by spring… that is providing the factory new engine didn't need an overhaul, the carburetor didn't need rebuilding, the fabric wasn't weak, the frame wasn't corroded, the instruments operated, and I remembered at least a portion of what I had learned in A&P school.

I eagerly looked inside the cylinders and any other orifice I could poke a gooseneck flashlight into. To my great relief, all that poking could not find any engine corrosion. Otis said he had faithfully pulled the engine through regularly and even had it borescoped several years ago. His diligence paid off because the engine appeared clean.

Originally I thought I could just replace the fuel and oil lines, test the carburetor, do some clean-up, build a lower cowl and go flying. Paint could come later. Nice plan, but a bit naive. Every time I took something off I found something else that either needed to be repaired, replaced, or rebuilt. I even discovered that, while the wings and tail feathers were covered with Ceconite, it had a cotton covered fuselage. It is amazing how easily fabric comes off an airframe. I found myself looking at a Pitts skeleton in no time.

The winter flew by. Almost every night and weekend were spent in the shop. It's not too hard to do when the wind is howling outside with forty below wind chills, and the snow is piling up. I would work away on the Pitts, dreaming of my first competition. The hardest part became motivating my body to get up out of the recliner to traverse the forty yards to the shop.

Almost every part was disassembled, inspected, painted, and put back in place. At first, I reluctantly defrocked the old girl but as I got to know her, I became more confident and nothing escaped my scrutiny. Floorboards, bungees, fuel lines, oil lines, tailwheel, rudder pedals, firewall, wings, tail feathers; I got into everything and enjoyed it all. Before I knew it spring had arrived and flying remained only a dream. I worked away into summer, pushing hard to get it into the air by the end of July for the Albert Lea contest. No luck! Even though I helped Larry Runge as an assistant starter for the contest, it was hard to sit and watch everyone else fly. Looking at all those gleaming airframes inspired me, and when I got home the sanding dust flew from determination to put a shine on my paint finish.

Near the first of October, Dick Weber and Larry Huston helped me haul the revitalized Pitts to the Buffalo airport where Terry and Susan Marsh were kind enough to let me use their heated maintenance hangar to put Humpty Dumpty back together again. On October 13, almost a year to the day from when N20DS and I were united, she lifted me off the runway, heart-pounding, knees shaking, and heading for the sky where we were both meant to be.

I know that there are many pilots out there who think competition aerobatic airplanes are just too darned expensive but I just proved them wrong. One thing I learned from sharing this experience with others is that there are a lot of neglected Pitts sitting around in the back of hangars waiting to be discovered. Many of them just need a little TLC. Some need a fairly major makeover like mine. The thing is, they can often be had for under $20,000. I have less than that in mine after all the work. That's the price of an ultralight! It will be a while before I compete in unlimited. When I get there, I will worry about a better airplane. In the meantime, Basic, Sportsman, Intermediate ... look out!

Afterlife

A leaf rustles out of sync with the slow dance of the bougainvillea plant as a breeze wafts through my screen. Two round marble eyes peek over the leaf's edge signaling a gecko about to emerge into the sunlight. The small, sleek lizard stops motionless for a moment and studies me before darting back into the bush. I wonder how long it has been alive. One year, five years, ten years? I know that it showed up a year ago because I watch its routine almost every morning as I sit on the glider in the lanai, sleepy-eyed, waking up from a night's rest. Lately, I've taken to pondering the string of events that brought the little guy to my back porch. Just like me, it had parents and those parents had parents, and their parents had parents, back to the beginning of time. If at any time, that chain had been broken, this little guy wouldn't be here.

For most of my life, I wrestled with the concept of life after death. Raised in a fundamentalist Christian home, I adopted the Biblical description of heaven. A clean and simple concept, there is a God who has prepared this wonderful place with no suffering or pain, and I can exist for eternity in pure bliss. I will live in a mansion with streets paved in gold and walls of precious stones. Of course, gold would have no value in heaven and even the most ornate mansion would become commonplace, if not dull after a little while. Not to mention the angels constantly chanting "Holy, Holy, Holy" and everyone bowing down before the throne continuously. Eternity is a long, long time. I have never been able to rationalize the whole thing. Secretly, the image did not sit well with me. Unfortunately, that came with the Christian package.

As I grew out of childhood, storybook images faded to be replaced by more mature observations of the real world. Still, those biblical accounts were there, unyielding. Christian apologists tried their best to make the image appealing but I continued to find it unsettling. I found it best to ignore those things that made me uncomfortable and not bring the subject up. Marriage produced children and the continuation of the faith that I had inherited. Faith in things unseen, as the Bible and pastors put it. A lot of good is contained in that faith but also more than a modicum of confusion. For years I studied the Word, confident that answers existed to my questions. Perhaps I didn't have the intellect to understand what was really being said. More often than not, I received the response that if I had enough faith I wouldn't need to understand. That didn't stop me from searching.

Now into my seventies, I sit contemplating a gecko. That seems simple enough but that little creature may offer a window into my afterlife. Every cell in its body, legs, head, and tail is an extension of its parents. I seriously doubt that it is thinking the same thing about me but I don't really know for sure. Who can? Whatever it is thinking is a product of generation upon generation before it. Even the plant it is perched on has a lineage going back to the first of its kind. "The first of its kind." Now there is a concept that I find impossible to get my head around. In all of my imagining, I can't conceive of a beginning—but that is a topic for another time.

For now, I'm focused on my existence beyond the grave and what this little creature might teach me. I had a recent conversation with friends concerning cremation. All agreed that the resulting ashes were not the person, only a small remnant—the loved one no longer existed except in memory. One friend placed a stone bench next to a lake in remembrance of a brother who had passed. My family has headstones in a graveyard. I know of friends and family members who believe in past lives, which would logically mean they believe in future lives as well. Then there are a variety of spirit world theories. I guess I am more of a pragmatist.

Back to the gecko. The question asked by all mankind is, what is life? I certainly can't begin to answer that one but I do know that, as a human, I tend to think in terms of consciousness. How would I know I'm alive if I wasn't aware of myself? Of course, that calls into question the six to eight hours a day I'm not conscious. I am alive but not aware. I guess that sort of applies to plants, too. I'm sure most people would like to be conscious of the fact they are alive. Geckos, too. So, when I die and lose consciousness, is my life truly over? I'm beginning not to think so. Not that I'm going to some shinning city in the sky but that my life lives on in my offspring. In fact, my afterlife began with the conception of my first child. Those cells that grew into my daughters are a continuation of me.

Geckos have an amazing feature. By whatever mechanism of design, they can regenerate parts of their bodies, primarily their tails. If a predator grabs them by their tail, it simply breaks off and within a month a new one will have grown in its place. I don't have that ability but I did have the ability to grow two whole new human beings, albeit with the help of my wife—essentially a living part of me. Now, this may seem obvious to most but the reality continues to grow in importance to me. DNA (deoxyribonucleic acid) is a fascinating subject, one that seems to be advancing in understanding rapidly. Just like my computer needs a program to function, DNA is the program that made me possible. My program is a combination of my father's and my mother's programs. The more scientists discover about DNA, the more intriguing it becomes. Every part of my body and my brain is a result of that program. I am a collection of generations going back to who knows when. Some part of every one of my ancestors lives within me and has been passed on to my children.

I have always cared deeply about my children's thoughts and feelings. I may not have been as observant as I should have or could have been. Life does have a way of getting in the way but that doesn't diminish the fact that what they are and who they are is extremely important to me. Like it or not, they are my afterlife. My girls are carrying me with them and I am a big influence on who they are, just as they are with their children. We may not agree on many things or view the world in the same way but those things are temporal in nature. The world is in a constant state of change as are our views and understanding. Those elements have their place of importance of course but underneath it all, we are all part of the same body. That doesn't change.

I don't know if that lines up with Biblical principles. It does have a familiar ring. My musings don't address the question of how this existence got started or where it will end. I would be remiss if I didn't acknowledge there appears to be a design behind it all, which may necessarily require a designer. That is far too great a mystery for my feeble brain. What I can grasp is this, just like the gecko, a part of me lives on in my offspring when my consciousness dies and my body turns to dust. Anything beyond that is anybody's guess.

Fly Away

He couldn't fly, simple as that. I've tried to teach him but he wouldn't learn. After years of coaching, he just didn't get it. Somehow the vision of floating effortlessly on the breeze completely eluded him. If he had just learned to fly he would have had so much more freedom.

When we first met, I didn't trust him. After all, I figured his bite could really do some damage and I didn't want to chance it. Of course, there were cage bars between us that made me feel a bit safer but feeding times got a little tense. I reached in and out of the dish as quickly as possible.

He seemed shy and reluctant to approach me. He'd hang back and watch. I don't know what was so entertaining. I simply sat there and stared back. I got the feeling that he lived a pretty boring life, all cooped up like that. Eat, drink, and stare... what kind of existence is that? I began to feel sorry for him.

Eventually, I got brave enough to approach him during feeding time–slowly at first with small movements. He would make little bird sounds to let me know he was concerned and hesitant. Each time, I got a little braver until one day he let me touch him. He didn't jump back or flinch. We each held our position for a few seconds and then I slowly backed away. That began a friendship that lasted years.

I decided to call him Bob. Don't ask me why. I don't know except that, "my friend Bob," sounded good—we were buddies. Bob sat around looking out the window a lot like he wished he could be out there. I got the feeling he wanted to sail over the city. We could see rooftops, busy streets, and crowded sidewalks from our window. I figured he could fly if he really wanted to but he just didn't have it in him.

If it wasn't for the television, I don't think Bob would have had anything interesting in his life. He could sit for hours watching the moving images on the screen. I tried to cheer him up. Sometimes I would sing to him. I don't have the greatest voice but he seemed to like it.

As time passed, we lost our fear of each other and I found I liked his company. We'd sit by the window together and watch the people below scurrying here and there with their busy lives. We wondered where they were going and why they were in such a hurry. Like me, Bob obviously didn't have anywhere to go or anybody to see. His life existed in our apartment. Sometimes I would find him talking to himself, kind of jabbering away and making no sense. I often wondered what he did when things went dark and I slept.

In the last few weeks, Bob became lethargic. He moped around, didn't eat much, and spent more time than usual gazing out the window. I could tell something was wrong but I didn't know what to do. He ignored my singing and kept his distance.

When I woke up this morning I found the window wide open and Bob was nowhere to be seen. I looked everywhere but he was gone. I waited all day for him to return but he didn't. By evening I was getting hungry. My dish was empty. Bob always filled my dish by this time.

Had he finally decided to soar out over the city?

Happy Birthday

"Happy Birthday to my Amazing Wife."

"To the One That I Love."

"To My Fabulous Wife!"

"To my lovely wife! Sending you love and kisses too, and hoping your birthday is as wonderful as you."

I really hate picking out cards. Whether for birthdays, Christmas, anniversaries, or whatever, I find it truly frustrating—particularly cards for my wife.

I pulled another card from the display featuring a cute cartoon couple on the front.

"Forget the past. You can't change it."

Forget the present. I didn't get you one.

Funny, but not appropriate.

Red hearts, roses, lace, pink bows, kissing silhouettes, and crazy cartoons—mush—how's a guy supposed to choose.

The card racks stretched on aisle after aisle. I had come to the Hallmark store next to Albertsons Grocery after spending way too much time in their card section with no luck. I figured that if I couldn't find one at the king of cards store, I would have to give up.

I am not a mushy romantic. My wife and I don't have cutesy names for each other like "sweety" or "dear" or "my little love muffin." She is Teresa, and that is what I call her. So picking out a card that says how much I care without getting all soft and gooey is a real challenge. But time raced on toward the party in a few hours. A choice had to be made.

Ah, here is one that might work, I thought

as I zeroed in on a card with swatches of pastel colors and devoid of flowers, hearts, or lace. The practical greeting had a simple list on the front.

"To my wife who is – Beautiful"

Yeah, I can live with that. She certainly is attractive. In fact, she isn't aware of how beautiful she is.

"Intelligent"

That is certainly true. I can have my desk covered in papers and she can spot the one typo seconds after walking in. She knows where our finances stand off the top of her head while I spend hours working the numbers. She reads constantly. *Yep, she's intelligent.*

"Trustworthy"

Whether it's the kids with a problem, friends needing help, or my emotional support, we can trust her to be there. And, never once, have I ever questioned her loyalty.

Trustworthy certainly applies.

"Caring"

By all means. Sometimes I think she is a bit too caring. She is deeply involved in the life of her family and friends. *Put a big check mark beside that one.*

"Helpful"

All too true. She is always there to help whenever asked, particularly when her kids or grandkids request it. Often to the point that I get volunteered in the process.

This card looks like the winner. I paid the outlandish $6.95 for the piece of paper and colored envelope and left Hallmark pleased with my choice.

Later that evening, with the family gathered around, my wife opened her presents to oohs and aahs. Three daughters, their families, and a few other relatives smiled gleefully as each present was revealed. Then came time for my present and card. She slid her finger under the lip of the pale blue envelope, pulled out the card, and began to read.

Her eyes got big and her mouth dropped open. Her hand went to her cheek as she let out a surprised, "whaaat?"

Two daughters looking over her shoulder cried out in unison, "Daa-aad!"

Confused by the unexpected response I answered, "what?"

"Why would you get a card like that for mom?" the eldest daughter fired at me.

"Like what? I thought it was a nice card."

"Nice? Do you even know what this card says?"

Totally confused, I'm sure my face showed it. "Yes, it says that your mom is beautiful, intelligent, trustworthy, caring, and helpful. What's wrong with that?"

"You really don't see what's wrong?" the second daughter chimed in.

"No, I don't." I reached for the card and took it from my shocked wife's hand. "Let me see that."

There was the list, just as I said—all good attributes—each one neatly lay below the other in attractive type. *Where the problem?* The puzzled look on my face signaled the others that I was totally oblivious to the problem right before my eyes.

"Look at the first letter in each word," the eldest daughter said.

There it jumped at me, spelled out vertically in bold letters, the beginning of each word. B-I-T-C-H

I felt flabbergasted. *How could it be?*

"This is a Hallmark card, I blurted out. "If you can't trust Hallmark, who can you trust?"

Seeing my surprise, the whole family burst out laughing. I tried to act nonchalant but couldn't conceal the red flush that warmed my cheeks. No doubt I would be hearing about this for many years to come.

I've Got It

Five thousand feet up, I could smell the sweet fragrance of eucalyptus trees lining the two-lane highway below. Chris and I had pushed the 150 horsepower Decathlon to that lofty height where we planned to practice inverted spins. Our designated aerobatic training area lay three miles west of the airfield over brown coastal hills that separated the Sonoma Valley from Petaluma. Blue skies and pleasant seventy-five degrees made it a perfect morning. San Pablo Bay gleamed in the early sun off to the south. A great day for seeing the sights, but we were up there to do some serious work.

Chris had an aerobatic competition coming up and wanted a second-party critique. I never passed up an opportunity to work on further developing my skills so we had arranged to trade-off flying the maneuver while the other observed. A good deal for me because, as an instructor, I spent most of my time in the back seat talking students through maneuvers rather than doing the flying. On this ride, I would not only fly but compare my ability to that of a seasoned aerobatic pilot.

Since Chris had rented the airplane with me as safety pilot, he served as "pilot in command." He sat in the front seat while I occupied my normal office in the back. With our slim-pack parachutes strapped on and five-point harnesses snuggly attaching us to the aircraft, we arrived at altitude ready for action.

"Okay, Chris, show me how it's done," I

chided into the headset microphone, knowing that he undoubtedly would outperform me.

"Sure enough. One inverted spin coming up," my headset crackled. "This one from inverted flight."

Chris slow-rolled the airplane upside down and held it. The loose ends of my shoulder harness straps floated toward the ceiling as my weight hung on the lap belt. He pulled the power back and eased the stick forward, slowing the Decathlon to a stall. Full forward stick, kick a rudder pedal, and the world overhead spun around. Looking up through the windshield, one, two, three times the road passed by, then Chris pulled the control stick back for a moment, kicked opposite rudder, forward stick and we flew out inverted. A quick half-roll and we were upright again.

"Nuts, I missed my point," came a disappointed voice from the front seat. "I didn't start my recovery soon enough."

Nose up, we climbed to gain altitude for another try.

"Your turn," Chris said. "You've got the airplane."

I took the controls, "I've got it," and did a few clearing turns to make sure we were alone in the sky. I rolled inverted and proceeded to follow Chris's example. The idea was to spin three rotations and stop on the same heading the maneuver started. My entry was okay but I made the recovery too soon and rolled out about twenty degrees off the entry point.

"Well, that's why we're here," I remarked feeling a bit disappointed that I hadn't impressed him with my airmanship.

After about twenty minutes of dueling spins, we both improved to where each spin entered and exited on point.

"What about trying a half-snap-roll entry to an inverted spin?" I asked. "I found that is a quick and easy way to enter. After all, it's basically a horizontal spin converted to a vertical spin."

"Sure. Sounds fun. You do one and I'll follow you through."

"Okay, I've got the airplane."

I set up, snap-rolled the plane to inverted, pushed forward, and entered the inverted spin, slick as could be, and then recovered after three turns.

"Now, that's fun," Chris's enthusiastic voice came over the headset. "My turn."

"You've got it."

For the next ten minutes, we traded off flying the maneuver. Chris quickly got the hang of it.

"That was perfect," I complimented as he rolled upright. "Time to head back. I've got a student at nine."

The airport lay off to the east only a few miles away and we were still at four thousand feet. I sat back and relaxed as Chris put the plane into a gentle descending turn away from the field.

Good, I thought, he is doing a slow letdown to cool the engine. Some pilots would pull the power back and dive for the airport, which could shock the engine after working it hard.

We chatted away about the spins, what we had done right and what we had done wrong while gently floating along in a shallow descent. As brown hills passed beneath the wings I marveled at the way trees and brush grew up the draws, leaving the crest barren. We circled out over the foothills toward Petaluma and then back toward the ridges that separated the two valleys. The morning air had not yet become turbulent so the airplane felt like my easy chair back home. This time, the hilltops were closer as we made our slow letdown. I figured Chris would pull the power back and head for the airport, but he opted to make one more circle. We cleared the tallest hilltop by about two hundred feet. I liked flying low. A couple of years as a crop duster and flying the Fish and Game Department counting wildlife got me hooked.

We cruised in an arc one last time out toward Petaluma and back to the hills. The grass-covered crest loomed ahead as we approached. Chris was on course for a low saddleback between two hills that were obviously above our altitude. Years of flying in the Rocky Mountains in low-powered Cubs and Champs had taught me how to judge whether I had the altitude to clear a pass. On one trip across Utah, I had my father, a WWII bomber pilot, flying from the front seat of my Aeronca Champ. He graduated top of his class as a bomber pilot, but was a nervous flier, particularly in small planes. As we approached a pass, I began to sense that we were two-hundred-feet too low to make it over. Not only that but in a minute or two, there would be no room to turn away. I had been watching a pair of hawks circling off to my right in the up-slope draft of our tailwind. With seconds to spare, I tapped Dad on the shoulder, yelled, "I got it," and slide the airplane in under the hawks. Up we went like we were in an elevator. That event became one of Dad's favorite flying stories.

Unfortunately, I didn't see any hawks to identify an elevator ride over these California hills as the pass rose in the windshield. I flashed back to a few months earlier when a guy I barely knew was giving a friend a ride in his WWII T-6. He had his friend flying the front seat when they smashed into these very hills, killing them both. I wasn't about to let that happen to us.

I really didn't want to offend Chris by criticizing his judgment. After all, he was an experienced pilot. But, if I didn't speak up, we were going to end our days as a grease spot on the side of that hill ahead. The brown grass came rushing at us at an alarming rate.

"Hey, Chris, I don't think you're going to clear that pass."

A shocked voice came blasting back over my headset. "ME. I thought you were flying!"

I yelled back, "I thought you were flying!"

I shoved the throttle all the way forward and pulled back on the stick. We both yelled, "I've got it!" at the same time.

Luckily, 150 horses with a constant speed prop made quick work of the altitude we needed to get over the pass but I swear we left tracks in the dirt.

With the ground dropping off on the other side, I called over the mic, "You've got it," and shook the control stick to make sure. In fact, we both had it.

"Yeah, I know I've got it."

"I'm off the controls," I reassured, and let go. "You've got it."

The short ride back to the airport passed quietly with only a few comments like, "that was too close for comfort, I can't believe we did that" and, "a rookie mistake."

Once on the ground, the incident became the joke of the day although we both knew it was far more serious. The "I've got it" stories came flooding out of the hangar-flying crowd, some comical and some downright scary. In the end, safety and proper cockpit procedure formed the bottom line of the conversation. Lots of opinions were shared on how to positively transfer pilot in command responsibility. Everyone agreed that a good shake of the stick by the pilot flying to let the other person know he/she had positive control was a good idea.

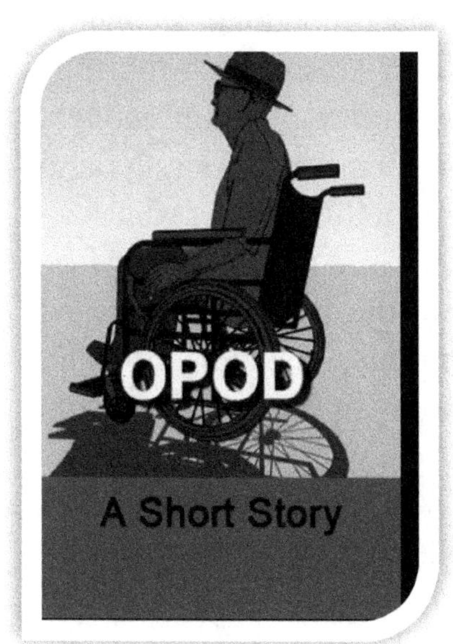

OPOD

About three months ago I began to suspect something wasn't right. We had just completed a move to Florida. The neighborhood appeared quite nice, well-groomed, with lots of palm trees and golf courses. The numerous ponds were beautiful and serene outside of the occasional sign warning "Gators Present." Sandhill cranes, perched atop slender legs, stood half as high as a man and squawked in unison each morning as the sun rose. Things were pleasant enough, and the people we met were friendly and cordial but I sensed something out of whack.

For some years, I noticed an unfamiliar face looking back at me in the mirror. Normally I don't pay much attention to the old gentleman as I get ready for the day but sometimes I stop and stare. I can't help wondering who the stranger is that hijacked my body and distorted it, almost beyond recognition. Maybe it's the new mirrors that came with the house. Particularly the medicine cabinet mirror mounted on an adjacent wall that, when set just so, reflects this strange person from the side, a perspective that has hitherto not been available to me. It appears that my rear has been lopped off and added to my front.

As if beginning my day staring at an old remnant of my former self isn't insult enough, I'm confronted with others suffering the same malady passing in a steady stream in front of my home in golf carts or walking tiny dogs. A trip to the store is no remedy. Aged faces, stooped shoulders, and flabby arms clutter every aisle. The drive to and fro requires special attention to avoid flattening some helpless little old lady behind the wheel of a boxy miniature vehicle that belongs on the cart path next to the 9th hole. Parking lots are fraught with peril as dim eyes and dim wits mindlessly back out of spaces without a thought of checking behind them.

Articles fill the local paper ads on dealing with the onslaught of aging. All sorts of ailments are just waiting to afflict the likes of me. There is an entire industry surrounding this community positioned to pounce on my every need - healthcare, dental work, insurance, transportation, hospitalization, housing, and food—all within the reach of a golf cart. Did I mention the frequent sirens from emergency vehicles, most prevalent in the early hours of the morning? I assume this is due to the frequency of old-timers not waking up after an evening's slumber.

This is, after all, an "active fifty-five plus community." I assumed, when we moved in, that we would find a range of folks from mid-life to advanced-age. Now it seems that the majority belong to the seventy and up variety to which I am, unfortunately, also a member. I find I may need to redefine the word, active.

"Get involved, join a club, take up an activity," I'm told. "Lawn bowling, bingo, bridge, crafts, model railroading – there are a ton of things to choose from."

So I did. I play pickleball several days a week, meet with a writers group, and even hang out at the local airport Friday mornings with a group of pilots, albeit mostly retired. Speaking of retired people, who has the time to do all those things mid-day all week long? People who are past their prime and have nothing better to do, that's who.

Don't get me wrong, they are mostly very nice people. In fact, some of my very best friends are old people just like me but I miss the faces, energy, and enthusiasm of young people. That's why I am beginning to suspect that I suffer from OPOD. I don't believe it is all that rare. In fact, I assume it may be quite common in this community, although seldom talked about. I'm not sure if there is a cure, at least if one remains in this locale. The affliction seems to be prevalent among Florida dwellers. I doubt that there is a medical treatment, and I suspect that it is fatal. I am particularly frustrated that I may be part of the problem.

I don't believe OPOD [Old People Over Dose] is contagious. Well, maybe just a little. The constant, day by day, hour by hour, contact with old people on every front reminds me that I am also old and not likely to get any younger. Those who seem oblivious to the malady can be influenced if it is brought to their attention. I never liked being the bearer of bad news but sometimes I just can't help myself.

Is there a remedy? I would like to think so. Unlike Juan Ponce De Leon, I am not seeking the fountain of youth. (For those who are history impaired, he was the first European to reach Florida). Denying the aging processes only provides a temporary reprieve. I suspect that finding a meaningful purpose, goal, or objective that diverts one's attention may be the best medicine. For some, that may be playing bingo eight hours a day. For me, I need to be productive, creative, and useful. The feeling that I may be irrelevant and I no longer have anything to contribute to society drains away my energy.

I am resolved to resist the onset of OPOD. I

will double down on my search for that next project or passion that adds meaning to life. Sitting on the porch in a rocker watching the sunset is nice, but only after a productive day of value.

Night Fright

Without warning, out of nothingness, a heavy weight on his chest trapped him to the ground. Before he could move, something ripped at his arm. He could feel his flesh tearing and hot blood rushing out, soaking into the flimsy material of his sleeping bag. He felt himself being lifted high into the air by hot fangs embedded in his shoulder. The smell of blood-dripping meat and animal musk pounded through his head. The ground came up at him hard but the slashing of claws through his chest made the blow to his head almost unnoticeable. His heart tried to rip its way out of his chest. His lungs lunged at the inrushing air.

With effort, he rolled himself over and opened his eyes for the first time... big and pulsating. The campfire dimly glowed with red-orange coals and beneath trees black with the feeling of death. His motorcycle and baggage were only a few steps away. He grabbed at his torn arm only to find it intact. The night lay silent. It had been a dream.

Heart pounding, he picked up his flashlight within easy reach, and probed and prodded the black night in every direction and then back again to those spots in the darkness that might conceal something. He tried hard to convince himself that nothing was out there.

Stars twinkled down on him from the safety of the sky. As long as he looked up at them, his heart rested and that dreaded overwhelming fear that engulfed his whole being would stay at his feet. He could sail up into the night sky while lying on his back and be in command of the entire universe. But, as soon as he lowered his eyes, an unholy something would rush around him and through him and terrorize his very soul.

He looked at the luminous hands on his watch and envied their ability to emit their own light. One A.M.—only a half-hour ago he had gone through a very similar light shining ceremony, stared at the stars pretending the forest wasn't there, and finally hiding in the depths of his sleeping bag in search of sleep.

Once again he burrowed into the sanctuary of his sleeping bag. As long as his thoughts were not allowed to stray beyond that soft, warm flannel, he could sleep. The familiar air inside smelled like home. He allowed his ears to hear a cricket chirp in the outside air, but nothing else. His thoughts reviewed the day's travels. The mountains were beautiful and the people friendly. Highways swung back and forth, following rivers, valleys, and up into the clouds over high, mountain passes. The day had been warm and moist with the aroma of fresh fields and trees.

A twig cracked through the stillness—a sound his ears couldn't ignore. Something was definitely out there. He struggled with himself over whether it was nothing or something to check out. The sleeping bag seemed so secure but a false sense at best. He would have to check.

His head slowly slipped out into the stiff night air. Wet grass and pine trees sent their greetings to him. Once again he performed the light shining ceremony. Nothing could be seen in the direction the sound had come and now he wasn't even sure if he had really heard the cracking twig. His light probed and prodded at the black trees and crossed over and over again, objects that took ominous shapes. He could see something vicious in every dark bump or odd-shaped lump. Fear began to creep at his head again. This time he would master it.

The light went out and the zipper of his sleeping bag traveled its zig-zag course down the copper track. The chilliness of the night air felt good against his skin. The soft forest floor gave with each step. All he could see were black shapes as he made his way toward the stand of trees that hid all the somethings. His heart thudded against his ears.

The farther away from the campsite he got,

the better he felt. He touched trees and twigs with his fingers and his toes. Ferns and tall grass brushed his legs with a gentle touch. An occasional sharp rock or stick would jab at him but his fault for not seeing them. Stars smiled through the trees as each dark something turned into logs, rocks, and bushes as he touched them. He wandered about probing with his hands at anything that looked suspicious. Everything became familiar.

The remaining coals of the fire guided him back to his sleeping bag. He slipped back in and pulled the zipper to the top. Warmth remained inside, almost as if he had never left. He hugged the flannel and smiled as he thought of what he had done. An experience like no other, he had met his fear face-to-face and licked it.

He found his comfortable place between the pebbles on the ground and took a deep breath. He allowed his ears to listen. Suddenly, his heart jumped.

Something is definitely out there!

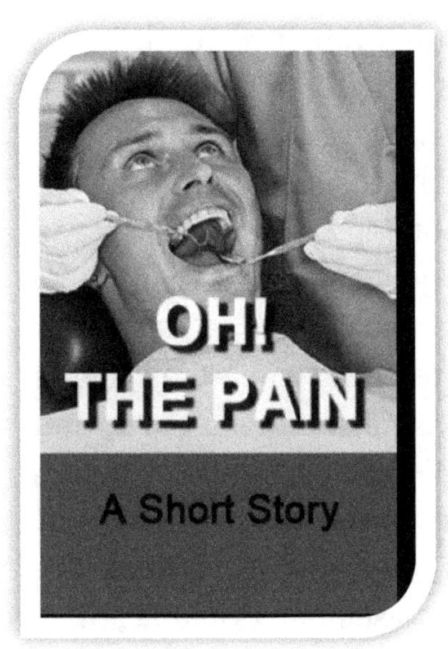

Oh, The Pain

Peter sat upright and stiff from tension, gripping the arms of the dentist chair as though trying to crush them. His face grimaced in terror. Unable to voice his fear, the twenty-four-year-old Russian's eyes pleaded with me to take him away. It took all the persuasion I could muster across a formidable language barrier to get him this far. He had bravely tried to mask the pain he was enduring caused by his inflamed tooth but it had become obvious something had to be done. I wasn't about to let him get out of that chair.

Several weeks earlier, Peter and his family arrived at our doorstep after a long and somewhat perilous journey from Chernobyl, then a member of the Soviet Union. The family of six included Peter, his wife, their small daughter, his father, and mother-in-law, and their teenage son. We agreed to host refugees but were a bit overwhelmed with the size of the family delivered to our home. Fortunately, we had a furnished basement available, with our eldest daughter away at college.

Stasko, their volunteer interpreter, unloaded the family from his van along with bundles of belongings, and introduced the small clan to us.

"I'm sorry they don't speak English except for Nadia, here," he pointed at the stoutly built, grey-haired lady. "She understands a little bit."

Nadia took a small step forward. "How you do," she said with a heavy Russian accent.

They all looked weary from their journey,

having just come from the airport after days of travel and wading through the jungles of bureaucracy on both sides of the ocean.

"Welcome to our home," I said, as I reached out to shake hands with the thin, pale patriarch standing at Nadia's side.

He smiled nervously and gave a small bow.

"Come in. We have lunch prepared for you," my wife said excitedly.

Stasko relayed our message as our new guests who were looking around, surveying our Minnesota five-acre hobby farm complete with barns, corral, and horse pasture. The family talked quietly among themselves with Nadia shaking her head, obviously in charge of the family. She then turned to Stasko and, in a very serious tone, unmistakable even in Russian, gave an ultimatum.

"Nadia says that they cannot accept a meal without first doing work. They must earn their food."

The family stood there, Daniel, Nadia, Peter, Svetlana, teenager Alexander, and three-year-old Marina, exhausted from their ordeal but immovable until I gave them some task to accomplish in payment for their first meal in our home. No amount of persuasion would change their minds.

I looked around at a loss for some simple work that could be performed. A small pile of old barn wood caught my attention. I had been meaning to move it to the center of the riding arena to burn.

"I suppose they could help me move that pile of wood, later," I said hesitantly to Stasko.

He pointed to the pile of wood and then to the arena, as he translated. Without hesitation the entire family, little Marina included, headed for the woodpile and began loading up arms full of worn, broken, and rotted remnants of farm history.

"No, no," I cried out. "After lunch."

"They say they must work first," Stasko said.

So their introduction to life in the land of plenty was as laborers. Daniel the elder, held up an old wormy worn piece of wood, and pleaded with his eyes, asking if he could save it. I told Stasko to let him know he was welcome to start a pile of his own, although I had no idea what he would ever do with junk wood. We experienced our first indication as to how hard their life in Ukraine had been. It appeared inconceivable to them that we would first, burn such a valuable resource, and second voluntarily share our home with no strings attached.

Several weeks had passed, and now Peter sat in abject fear of the dentist who had left the room to study the x-rays he had taken. The young man's fear seemed extreme. I am not a fan of the dentist either but I had never seen anyone recoil so intensely over an encounter with the tooth doctor.

"No problem, Peter," I encouraged. "No problem."

"No, No. Big, big problem," Peter said while maintaining a vice grip on the vinyl-bound chair arms.

"Why?" I shrugged.

Over the next few minutes, Peter unfolded his tale through a few words and a lot of pantomimes.

"Me Russian Army," he said as he gave a salute. He opened his mouth wide and pointed to a missing molar deep in his jaw.

I watched as he demonstrated the best he could how the army surgeon put a knee to his chest, took a hammer and chisel, and proceeded to remove his tooth in chunks with no numbing medicine whatsoever. The surgeon's assistant pinned down his arms so he couldn't resist.

Peter held his jaw and made a face in severe pain. "Ooooh, no good, no good."

"No problem here." I tried to reassure him as I shook my head and waved my hands in front of me. He wasn't buying it.

The dentist returned to administer Novocain around the infected tooth. Peter bravely allowed the doctor to work, his eyes betraying his deep-seated fear. As the minutes passed and the numbing spread, he patted his cheek in wonder.

The doctor came back again, this time picking up the extraction tools placed there by his assistant. Peter's eyes grew large in anticipation of the extreme torture that was about to take place. He looked at me with darting glances of confusion that seemed to say, "Have you betrayed me?"

With tools in hand, the dentist reached in, gave a few tugs, withdrew the bloody offending cuspid, and dropped it in the stainless steel tray next to Peter's elbow. A quick rinse with the water tube, a spit, some packing, and it was all over.

Peter looked at the tooth, then up at me, and shrugged his shoulders with an, "Is that all there is?" expression.

"All done," the doctor said with a smile.

Peter beamed. "Nooooo problem!" He then added, "America, excellent!"

I found Peter a good job in a cabinet shop. After a few very interesting months of living in our basement, the family got their own apartment and started their new life in a new country. A few year passed before they chose to move south to Florida where a large Ukrainian community resided. We moved west to the Rocky Mountains and lost touch with our Russian friends. That is until a week ago.

"Dad, guess what! I found Peter!" My daughter's excited voice came across my cell phone loud and clear. "Peter Gavrilenko."

"You did? How?" My enthusiasm surprised me.

"On FaceBook. I found his page on FaceBook."

That began a process that eventually led to a phone conversation with the young man who had trusted me enough to sit in the torture chair. He had raised a family, owned his own business, and broke into tears when we found him again. We reminisced until his emotion overcame him and he couldn't talk anymore.

That conversation has just begun the next chapter in a bond created between two families that shared a special time together—a time that changed the lives of all involved.

Reunion

Memories are already fading
faces too briefly seen
encounters with old friends
and friends that might have been

stories of long ago
days of youth remembered
feelings so long forgotten
re-emerge in life's December

for one brief moment in time
for one short weekend of days
a step taken back in time
a step far back in haze

a half-century melts away
along with creases and lines
young faces emerge from old
remembering all the good times

but life has a way of returning
when all the fanfare is gone
when daily life sets upon us
and a new day finally dawns

it's a time we won't forget
that time we journeyed back
when we laughed and hugged each other
yet having traveled a different track

what we shared as a common bond
was so far in the distant past
best kept in this brief encounter
added to memories that last

too much familiar exposure
and old faces return once more
it was nice to encounter youth for a moment
but life exposes reality's core

we have all grown so much older
and have experienced triumphs and trials
too much nostalgic pondering
dulls those initial smiles

like the taste of fine wine
that leaves you wanting more
a brief weekend encounter
is a taste of what's in store

so friends new and old
wonderful to reunite with you all
perhaps in year five or ten
we will have another reunion ball

BOOKS BY LAWRENCE V. DRAKE

Pilots & Painted Ladies: 493rd Bomb Squadron and the Air War in the CBI

Schellville: The Aviator and the Hippie

Red Boots Rebel: Keeping Secrets

When Silence Calls: Freeing the Island Deaf

The Entrepreneur Experience: Good Choices and Common Mistakes

Visit DrakeIP.com or scan the code below.

www.ingramcontent.com/pod-product-compliance
Lightning Source LLC
La Vergne TN
LVHW050639100826
845148LV00011B/1916

* 9 7 9 8 9 8 5 4 0 4 0 5 0 *